THE DIAMOND GUARDIANS

Talin Mari

Talin Mari Books
www.TalinMari.com

Book 1 of The Diamond Guardians Series

My heart binds this book, but without these

people, my book would not have a soul:

I want to thank my husband and children for believing in me.

They are the roots that hold me together.

They are the ones that let my imagination run wild.

I want to thank my family for their encouragement.

They have given me the gift of education.

I want to thank my friends for letting me be who I am,

without any prejudice.

I want to thank you for reading my story.

The day everything changed...

CHAPTER ONE

I was no longer a girl who lived in the mountains of Topanga.

We had only been in school for a week and I had already started to get used to classes. The teachers had gone through their introductory speeches and had taken care of their logistical duties for the classes, such as "adds" and "drops".

My favorite teacher was my *Intro to Politics* teacher, Professor Smith. He seemed so dynamic. I wanted to drop everything and intently listen to him when he spoke.

"Good morning class," said Professor Smith.

"Khem... khem," he said while clearing the phlegm in his throat. Professor Smith was looking down at his notes to start the lecture.

"Let's start off by talking about the concept of having a political system...," continued Professor Smith as he clasped his hands.

I got ready to write down notes on the lecture. I was worried that if I forgot one word, I would be regretting it during exam time.

"Who knows why we should even have a political system?" asked Professor Smith. "Yes... I believe your name is David Blaze." Professor Smith looked down at his paper to make sure he had the right last name.

"I think it's so that we don't have chaos," replied David.

David's voice made my body tingle. It was as if I fell in love with a voice. My breath slowed down and I was blushing. Why? It wasn't like he had even spoken to me. I couldn't think. I desperately wanted to leave because I felt like everyone would know how I felt. I didn't even turn back to see how this person with the charismatic voice looked like. It's silly to feel this way about a voice, isn't it?

Once class was over, which felt like a lifetime, I quickly gathered my books and ran out of class.

"Is this your pen?" asked the voice as I scurried quickly down the hall.

I didn't want to turn back. I was worried that the image would not measure up to the beauty of David's voice. I slowly turned around, fretting every moment. My heart pounded faster with every turn.

"Um… yeah," I said as I slowly moved my eyes away from the pen in his hands and towards his deep brown eyes. His thick lashes shaded his bold brown eyes.

"I must've dropped it," I added.

I slowly and clumsily walked towards David, the guy with the charismatic voice.

"It's a nice pen," David said, trying to make small talk.

"Yeah… um… thanks for picking it up," I said blushing.

I grabbed the pen, but couldn't stop looking at his eyes and curled lashes.

"My name's David."

"Yeah… I figured. I mean, Professor Smith called on you in class." I was starting to tremble. My voice sounded like a cell phone conversation that would continuously get disconnected.

"Um… my name is Katrina Swan."

I took out my right hand to shake his hand. I was breaking out into a sweat. His thick hands were as soft, yet commanding, and mine were sweaty and shaky. My stomach was starting to hurt. I didn't know if it was my nerves or the lunch that I had eaten earlier.

"It's nice to meet you… Katrina," David said. "Um… hey, do you like this class?"

"It's my favorite. I've heard so many good things about Professor Smith," I said, finally having gained confidence in my voice and appearance.

"How about you?"

"It's okay," he replied. "I'm not sure what I want to major in, but I thought I'd try to see if I'd like this class."

"I've heard from people in my dorm that he's supposed to be great.... Um... he called me before I came here. He's supposed to be my academic advisor," I said while starting to get nervous again.

"Really? I didn't pick a major," said David. "Maybe that's why no one called me," he laughed.

"Well, I've got to go to my next class.... It was nice meeting you. I'll see you around," said David as he turned back to look at me. His eye lashes fluttered up and down like soft feathers brushing up against his bold eyes. His powerful eyes muted his beautiful golden blonde hair.

My heart raced. I was on the verge of passing out! My knees trembled and my mind was drawing a blank. After David left, I felt like everyone was staring at me. I felt like a fool for not having had a real conversation with him. I could barely stand up and look like I wasn't about to crumble.

My stomach was starting to hurt even more now that David had left.

"Hey! Is everything alright?" asked Amber. She was walking down the hallway.

"You look like you're gonna pass out," said Amber.

Amber was my neighbor in my dorm. She was the first person I met when I came to Occidental College. She was a social city girl who had been raised in San Francisco. I, on the other hand, was raised and homeschooled with little social interaction in the mountainous community of Topanga, which is in the outskirts of Los Angeles. We somehow made our differences work.

"Come on," continued Amber. "I think you need to go lie down in your room."

Amber looked really worried.

"I feel fine. My stomach just hurts a little…. I think I'll be fine…. really." I tried to convince myself.

"I just need to get out of here," I cried as I tried to convince myself that everything was alright.

"Wait up!" yelled Amber.

I started running to my dorm room. Amber was running after me.

"Let me at least carry your books," she said in the distance.

She wouldn't leave me alone. I didn't care about my books. I felt weird. Something was not right. I just needed to be alone.

I got to my dorm room and slammed the door shut.

"Katrina! Open the door!" yelled Amber.

"Just go away…. I'm fine. I don't know why you followed me here…. I'm fine on my own," I said.

I didn't want anyone to see me while I was in complete and utter pain.

I fell into a deep trance, reenacting the events that had occurred in the class. I couldn't stop thinking about David, the voice that had a name and a face. But, the pain didn't go away. It only got worse as I thought of David with his charismatic voice and his captivating eyes.

My head started to spin. At the same time, I felt like there was a needle piercing my abdomen.

Nothing seemed to matter anymore. Not David. Not Amber.

"Katrina! You need to open the door. Why are you hiding from me? What's going on with you?" Amber said. She would not leave me alone. She was continuously pounding on the door.

"I'm fine. Just leave! I need to go to sleep!" I yelled back.

I didn't want Amber to see me in complete agony.

I took a deep breath. It became heavier with each moment. My lungs seemed to radiate with the air that filled within it. I ran to my mirror and saw strands of my hair changing color. One by one, an inch of my hair became golden. Was I going crazy? Was it something that I had eaten at lunch? Where did my dark brown hair go?

With each strand of hair, I felt like I knew what others felt. I did not know what they were thinking, but rather what they were feeling.

I could hear the door pounding harder.

"Amber… really… I'm fine. Just leave!" I said, really getting annoyed at her insistence to see me.

"Katrina, if you don't open this door, I'm going to call Campus Security," demanded Amber.

"Are you on meds or something? Come on… tell me. I'm your friend," she cried out.

"No. I'm fine. I keep telling you I'm fine. I just have the stomach flu or something," I tried to say convincingly.

I didn't know what to do. I ran into my bathroom to try and scrub off the golden color off of my hair. Unfortunately, there was nothing I could do! I couldn't figure out what I had done to have caused my hair to change color. There must have been a scientific reason. I'm sure it was all in my head.

The door kept on pounding! Louder and louder!

I started to cry. I went from a moment of complete bliss, having met a man with a voice that magnified my senses, to now not knowing what had happened.

The tears continuously fell like a steady stream on my reddened face. What could I do? How could I stop everything? My stomach kept on hurting. The stabbing pain in my abdomen continued to radiate my body. With each stab in my stomach, I saw another strand of golden hair. It was a never ending cycle.

I got a towel from the bathroom and wrapped my hair so that Amber wouldn't see the different color.

"See!" I exclaimed as I opened the door with my reddish face.

"There's nothing wrong with me. I'm just a little sick with the stomach flu. I'm okay, really," I tried to tell Amber.

"You don't look like you're okay. You really need to go to the Health Office," said Amber.

"I don't want to leave," I added.

"I'm sure the Health Office can give you something to stop the stomach flu," insisted Amber.

"I don't think they can help me," I said hopelessly.

"I'm sure they can," Amber comforted me as she put her hand around my shoulder. "Maybe they can give you some anti-nausea med."

"Amber, I'm not going," I asserted. Amber didn't know that my real problem was not my stomach ache, but the changes that were happening to my body and my hair.

"Fine…. I'll go see if there's something at the bookstore. Don't leave!" she commanded.

I shut the door as she left. I was happy that I could revel in my own misery without Amber and without her knowing of my transformation.

Finally, the pain stopped. I managed to grasp some air after having cried for such a long time. I looked like I had streaks of light golden highlights. There wasn't any way that I would be able to cover up my new hairdo. I knew I couldn't hide it from everyone. The odd thing was that it actually looked like streaks of real gold in my hair.

CHAPTER TWO

I walked into Statistics class, hoping to be discreet. Luckily, I had arrived there early enough so that I could avoid Amber. I made a point of finding a seat in a corner of the room to make it hard for anyone to find me. I had a dark blue cap on so that the golden sparkles in my hair would not be noticeable in class.

Amber walked in and looked for a seat. I could tell that she was looking for me, but I made no effort to let her know where I was. She sat down and kept on looking around for me.

I put my head down and pretended to be writing something. I wanted my cap to cover my face. I didn't want to have to explain my new hair color to Amber. After all, I have no idea what had happened to me and she was freaking out at my door until I managed to get rid of her.

The class had not yet started when I heard David's charismatic voice gently creep up behind me.

"Is this seat taken?" asked David.

"Where did you come from?" I asked in a very surprised tone. I started to feel my stomach hurt again. Was he the cause?

"I know that it's starting for you," said David very calmly.

"What's starting? What are you talking about?" I asked with my face turning blue from the immense pain I was feeling. I knew that my hair was starting to change color as well.

"We really need to talk," whispered David as he leaned over.

"I don't want to talk and I don't know what you mean about something starting for me," I said.

"It's really important!" insisted David.

"No," I said assertively, trying to ignore David's face and looking in front of me.

Within moments of hearing David's voice and seeing him sit next to me, I started to feel different. I could feel the emotions of the other students in class. The brown haired boy in the front row was upset because he had gotten off the phone with his parents who didn't want to buy him a car. The black haired girl behind him felt so happy to be seated next to the blonde haired boy, whom she had met in her residence hall. Amber felt confused and rejected because she couldn't find me. She was wondering if I was still sick in my room. It was so overwhelming that my stomach couldn't stop hurting.

"I need to go!" I exclaimed to David as I ran out of the room.

"Stop! Katrina!" yelled David.

Everyone in class turned and looked, including Amber. I didn't look back and ran to the quad.

I kept on running endlessly. I didn't know where I was going, but I knew I needed to get away from David. I'm sure he was the reason for all of my agony.

"Get away from me!" I yelled at David who was following me. "I don't know what you're doing to me."

"I'm not doing anything to you," he responded. "I promise. It's not me."

"I don't believe you! Just get away," I commanded while running away from him.

"You can't keep running," David said panting.

"Leave me alone. This is all your fault," I continued.

"Please… stop! It's not me!" pleaded David.

I stopped running and turned back to look at David.

"Then, if it's not you, who is it?" I asked David.

"It's no one. It's just the transformation. We all go through it. I promise it won't be so bad in a couple of days," he said as if he was almost begging me to forgive him for my agony.

"What are you talking about?" I asked.

"Let's go to the Sycamore Glen and I'll explain it to you there," said David in his beautifully crafted voice.

The Sycamore Glen was a secluded part of the campus that was green and lush, surrounded by aged trees and bushes. The school hosted parties at the Sycamore Glen. I hadn't been to one, so going there

16

was a novelty to me. However, the thought of going there alone with David made me nervous. I didn't know much about him.

"How do I know that you aren't going to put me under some sort of spell?" I asked.

"What! Do you think I'm a witch? Yeah... right!" David laughed.

"I don't think so," he huffed with a small grin.

"Then why is it that every time I hear your voice or even think of you, my stomach hurts like I have a knife stabbing it over and over again?"

"I'll explain everything to you. Just follow me to the Sycamore Glen," he responded.

The pain in my stomach magnified each time I got upset with David. Any thought of him made it worse.

"Come on," said David. "We have to talk in private. Let's go. No one will see or hear us there. I promise not to put you under a spell." David gave off a small giggle as he spoke of the spell.

"I guess… I really don't have any choice," I replied.

I walked slowly to the secluded hilly part of school.

The Sycamore Glen looked like a forest, reminiscent of my home in Topanga. The weeping willows drooped so low as if to kiss the ground beneath them. I could hear the rustling of the dried up leaves that I stepped on while inching towards the center of the green heaven.

With all the pain that I was going through, even the smell of the sweet trees did not comfort me. I wanted to find out what David was about to tell me. Maybe it would help me get rid of the pain.

"Here… why don't you sit down on this bench," David said.

I sat down on an old park table bench. It looked like it was as old as Occidental College itself. The bench was discolored with uneven edges. It had a beautiful sense of character to it like the rest of the school.

I started to feel dizzy. I think the pain had really started to affect my energy. With every shooting cramp, I could feel another strand of hair turning gold. It was endless. Unfortunately, it felt like the cramps were intensifying and the golden strands of hair were multiplying rapidly.

"It's ok, Katrina. We all go through this," said David in the most comforting voice as he sat next to me with his arms around my shoulders.

"I'm surprised that your parents never talked to you about this," continued David. "I knew that this was coming when I turned fifteen years old."

"It really is natural," said David as he stroked his hand up and down my shoulders.

I gave him the most vicious look anyone could give another living soul.

"Natural!" I yelled. I threw off his hand from my shoulder with disgust. "What's so natural about having golden hair grow every time I have a cramp in my stomach? I know I'm not imagining things! I know I could feel everything that the other students felt when I walked into our class today."

"Don't worry. It's normal," he replied.

"This isn't normal. Stop saying that! And, what's this about my parents? How do you know they know about this?" I asked with one sentence sounding faster than the other.

I had so many questions. I was asking them in a fury without any care that I was in the utmost physical pain.

"I promise it will get better. My hair wasn't blonde either. My transformation happened when I was seventeen years old," responded David very calmly.

David paused for a moment and stood up. He started to pace around in front of me.

"What's this transformation that you keep talking about?" I asked, frustrated that I wasn't getting anywhere with the conversation.

"All of our parents know about our transformation. I'm surprised you haven't had the talk yet," he said again nervously, while starting to pace faster in deep thought.

"My dad isn't alive," I said crying. "How could he tell me? And... my mom, well, she's too busy drowning her tears in her artwork to even talk to me."

He stopped pacing and gathered his thoughts so that he could give me '*the talk*'.

"I'm sorry.... I didn't know.... um... I'll tell you about it," he added.

"The transformation is a rite of passage. There's three phases. In the first phase, you'll meet your partner or someone from our people. For you, it happens to be me. In the second phase, you end up being in a lot of pain while your hair color starts to change. However, at the same time, you begin developing your powers. In the final phase, you'll know what your powers are and how to use them," said David.

"Are you telling me that we're some sort of freak?" I asked.

"Not really. I mean, we aren't freaks… we… we're superhuman," he added.

I gasped.

"This is a practical joke, right?" I asked. "Is Robbie in on this?"

"Who's Robbie?" asked David.

"He's a friend of mine from where I grew up…. Hm… it's got to be Amber," I was thinking out loud while holding my hand to my stomach.

"No one put me up to anything," insisted David. "Look… the world's not going to be the same for you. Nothing you can do will ever change the way you are now. You're going to have powers that other people only dream of having."

"What kind of powers?" I asked.

"I don't know. Everyone's different. You'll find out during the transformation," he added.

I was silent as David spoke. His charismatic voice seemed to enhance the importance of what he was explaining.

David continued, "You know how I was saying that someone who's your partner can trigger the transformation."

"Yeah," I replied.

"Well, I'm your partner. We're supposed to always protect each other. My mom told me that finding my partner is like finding my other half."

"What are you talking about David? This is all just a joke. How do you know that I'm your person or partner or whatever it's called?" I asked.

"Look at the symbol behind my neck," David insisted.

I looked behind his neck and found a golden star with an illuminating silver diamond in the middle.

"You have one too," explained David. "Just look in the mirror when you get back. Since we have the same symbol, it means that I will be able to feel what you feel and vice versa. We will always protect each other. Others of our kind have the golden stars too, but the diamond in the middle are a different color. There are no more than two identical stars."

Now, I finally understood why I had been so drawn to David, even without having seen his face, his voice had captivated me.

"Can people tell that I'm different?" I asked.

"You don't look different to them. Your hair color isn't golden when they see you. It's just a natural blonde. They also don't see your symbol on your neck. They'll think that you're different because you'll be hiding our secret and acting weird because of it... whether that's good or bad," he answered.

We both drew to a silence.

"Let's get back," said David. "You've already started the second phase and really need to rest."

He had done most of the talking, but I felt drained from all my pain and new found knowledge. I desperately wanted to get back to my room and take a nap. I was hoping that it was all a bad dream. I wanted everything to go back to the way that it was before my nightmare had started.

CHAPTER THREE

The second phase of the transformation was the most painful. After having left the Sycamore Glen, my body started to feel faint. I was numb from all the pain. I went straight to my dorm room.

"Amber, what are you doing here?" I asked.

Amber was waiting impatiently in front of my door.

"I wanted to know what happened to you," said Amber in a very bossy tone. "You totally ignored me in class and, then, ran out like the world was about to fall apart!"

"I don't know how to explain everything. I can't even figure it out myself," I said.

I felt really guilty, but I didn't know what to say. Besides, the numbing pain in my stomach made me want to push her aside, open my door, and crawl into my bed.

"Does this have anything to do with David?" she asked. "I heard he's really popular with the girls on campus."

"It's not like that," I assured her. "There's nothing going on between us."

"Is that why you stormed out of class while he ran after you?" asked Amber.

"It's just complicated," I tried to justify my actions. "Besides, David hasn't done anything to me. I really don't know what your problem is with him."

"Why were you running away from him?" she asked.

"I can't explain it…. um…. It's me. I'm the problem. He hasn't done anything to me other than try to be nice. I'm the one who's having issues," I said without revealing what my real issue happened to be.

"I'm really tired," I said, sounding very annoyed by her bossy disposition.

"What happened to your hair?" asked Amber. I ignored her.

All I could hear from Amber was nagging background noises.

I gently moved Amber to the side as I unlocked my dorm's door knob. My head was feeling dizzy. I slowly walked into my room, ignoring all the chattering noises I could hear from her. Nothing seemed to matter anymore. I blocked her out. The room seemed to rock. All I could hear was "hair", "why", and, then "doctor", "okay". None of the words Amber said were coherent to me.

I headed straight to my bed and fell on it like I was a leaf that naturally fell to the floor. That was when I went into an unconscious state of sleep.

When I woke up, I felt two people holding my hands. One was very small and slender and the other was soft and large. I slowly opened my eyes and saw Amber and David, each on the opposite side of my bed.

"Katrina," whispered David. "You're going to be all right. It just takes patience."

He stroked my hands very gently with his large, gentle hands.

"It's okay Katrina," explained Amber. "David told me everything."

What? Why did David expose my most embarrassing secret? I was trying to hide everything from Amber and now I was exposed.

"David. Why?" I couldn't say more.

The pain still numbed my entire body. My stomach still ached. It felt like needles constantly piercing my stomach. Each time my brown curly hair turned golden, it felt like someone was plucking out a strand of my hair. As each minute passed by, it felt like there was more than one strand transforming to the new color.

"Don't worry. Amber's one of us," replied David.

"Yeah… I don't have the golden hair you guys have, but I do have the shiny blue eyes…. I'm a little different than your kind of people, but we work together."

It was no wonder that Amber's eyes were such a brilliant blue color, one that I had never seen before I had met her.

"Katrina, I couldn't leave you alone on your first day of transformation. I came to your room and found Amber next to you. When I looked behind her neck as she leaned next to you, I saw a blue diamond on her neck. She's one of us," added David.

I didn't know if I should be happy because there were others too or if I should cry from the pain.

"My transformation happened when I was seventeen," said Amber. "It's easier when it happens at home because our parent's know what to do. Unfortunately, you're stuck with us."

"My mom," I said curtly.

"Your mom can't help you now," Amber abruptly interrupted. "She could have only helped you decrease your pain when it had just started. You've been transforming for several hours now. There's nothing anyone can give you at this point."

I started to cry. I was all alone as I had always been. I was suffering and no one could do anything to help me.

"We're here for you," continued David. "Katrina... Katrina... Katrina."

I could hear David, but I didn't feel like saying anything.

"It's almost over," said Amber. "The rest is easy."

Those were my favorite words as I stared into the eyes of my blue eyed friend, Amber. Her blue crystal-like eyes now made sense to me. It was like a puzzle that I was finally able to figure out. Everything was finally making sense. Maybe I was destined to meet Amber and, as for David, it must have been our natural pull together that had brought us to Occidental.

"You just have a few more strands of hair left," continued Amber.

"Why is my stomach hurting so much if it's my hair that's changing color?" I asked feeling pure agony from everything that I was going through.

30

"Well, it's because our body parts are all connected," said David sounding scholarly.

Honestly, what he said didn't explain anything. You don't need to be a rocket scientist to know that your body parts are connected.

I didn't bother asking more questions. There was no point. It's not like Amber and David knew what to expect. They had transformed within the past few years. They were looking for answers just like I was.

Finally, the pain slowly went away. I got out of bed gently, afraid that one wrong movement would make it come back again. The odd thing was that I didn't even break out in a sweat after the hours of pure agony. The pain was now gone!

"That's it! You made it!" cried Amber. "The couple of days of the transformation aren't even going to compare to what you went through."

I ran to the mirror, thinking that I may have turned into some form of a monster.

"Wow! Is that me?" I questioned myself. I touched the mirror in disbelief. My hair looked like a golden treasure. Within all the golden strands, I could see a few strands of my old brown wavy hair. Oh, how I missed it! They were now only reminders of who I used to be.

I flipped my hair to the side and saw the star on my neck shining brightly. I softly stroked it, worrying that I may ruin its beautiful appearance. Other than the golden hair and the star on my neck, I looked the same. However, it felt like there was something else that was different about my body. I pulled up my shirt slightly and found that there was a yellow half diamond next to my belly button.

"See... I told you that our body is connected," said David with a snicker and a slight smile. "I have the other half of your diamond." David showed his illuminating half diamond by taking off his shirt.

"Okay. This is getting to be too gross," laughed Amber. "I need to get out of here."

Amber felt like she happened to be in the wrong place at the right time.

David laughed.

He put his shirt back on and walked towards the door.

"Good luck with the rest of it. I'll see you when it's all over, if I don't see you in class," David said with his charismatic voice.

David took large strides as he walked out of the room. His job seemed to be done because he had made sure that his *'partner'* had survived the second phase of the transformation.

"I'm sorry you're stuck with him," added Amber after David left. "He seems like a jerk. I hope my partner isn't like him."

I didn't feel the same way as Amber. David's voice captivated me and his eyes made my heart melt. Nonetheless, he was the reason for my transformation as far as I was concerned. So, he was strictly off limits. This was going to be a business partnership.

Just because we were *'partners'*, it didn't mean that we had to like each other.

"You haven't found your partner?" I asked Amber.

"No. I've been looking for him, but I can't feel him yet," replied Amber.

"Why did you decide to come to Oxy?" I asked. I had gotten use to the jargon that Oxy was slang for Occidental College.

I continued, "I mean… I felt like I needed to be here. I thought it was because of all the beautiful greenery and the fact that it's like a green paradise in the middle of a bustling city, but I really don't know if that's the real reason anymore…. It seems like it was just meant to be. I think I was meant to meet David."

Amber paused for a moment to really think about why she decided to attend Occidental College.

"I don't know why I decided to come here. I got into U.C. Berkley too, but it didn't seem to be the right fit," responded Amber.

Amber naturally fell onto my chair and rocked from side to side thinking.

"I don't know," whispered Amber again.

"Do you think I'm your reason for coming here?" I asked.

"I don't know. I mean, my brother went to Brown University... I could have gone to the East Coast too, but it didn't seem right," said Amber.

"Maybe your partner goes to Oxy too," I responded. "I could have gone to UCLA with my friend Robbie, but I just couldn't confirm my acceptance.... Something stopped me.... David stopped me."

All of a sudden, I felt discomfort, not physical, but emotional. I didn't know what to do and wanted to be left alone. I was feeling overwhelmed with everything that had happened to me and was starting to panic.

I needed to have Amber leave so that I could calm myself down and see what I had actually become. I finally gathered my nerves to ask her to leave.

"Amber, I'm really tired," I said almost reluctantly because I didn't know how she would react to me asking her to leave. "I really need to sleep."

"Sure," replied Amber.

"Let me know if you need me. I'll hear you from my room if you yell!" she said as she laughed her way out the door.

Amber's dorm room was below my room. She was the first person I had met and the one who helped me move in. My mom hadn't come out to help me move in and my father passed away a year ago from a heart attack. I don't even know how it happened because the paramedics had taken him away even before I got back from my hike in the hills of Topanga that day. My mom told me that he was dead. She ignored me most of the year, drowning herself in her artwork.

Finally, there was no one around. I ran to the mirror to stare at my new self again. I didn't know what the third phase of the transformation would hold for me, but at least, the worst was over.

CHAPTER FOUR

I woke up ready to face more of my transformation. I was hoping that I had finished my second phase because I felt normal. The thought of going to class rather than waiting for any unexpected events from my transformation was appealing. I went to my bathroom anxiously wondering if my hair color was still golden.

As I walked into the bathroom to wash my face and brush my teeth, my heart was beating rapidly. Maybe, I was dreaming. Maybe, everything that had happened yesterday was only a dream. I didn't know if I should really look in the mirror. I lowered my head, trying to avoid the uncertainties of the mirror.

When I got to the sink, my curiosity overtook my anxiety and I slowly raised my head to look. My golden colored hair was still there. It looked beautiful! I still had streaks of my old brown color, but the powerful gold outshined any of the old hair color.

Quickly, I went back to my room excited that I had not imagined anything that had happened to me the prior day. I wasn't going crazy. The pain had vanished and I was left with a beautiful set of golden highlights in my hair. I was curious about my new powers and what they would be.

I eagerly got ready to leave my room. It was liberating that I no longer had any pain. I put on a pair of jeans, a t-shirt and low-cut boots. My wavy golden hair hung effortlessly down my back. I didn't bother to do much with it so that I wouldn't waste time before eating breakfast.

Someone knocked on my door. It was Amber, which was what I had anticipated.

"Ready to go to breakfast," Amber said cheerfully.

She was always so happy when she saw me. She made a point of saying "hi" to everyone with a beautiful smile. I knew it wasn't only me that she was happy to see. Everyone loved her sociable demeanor.

"Sure. Why don't we go somewhere to get a small bite to eat? I'm not in the mood of going to the cafeteria," I said.

"Do you want to go to the Samuelson Pavilion for breakfast?" Amber asked.

"That's fine with me," I replied without any hesitation. I desperately wanted to leave. I was in my room most of yesterday and needed to go outside.

The Samuelson Pavilion was a coffee shop hangout for students that also served muffins and other quick breakfast bites. It was nice to get away from my room for a while.

"You know, the second day isn't going to be so bad. It's just going to be very strange," Amber remarked as we walked to the Pavilion for a quick morning bite.

"There's going to be odd discoveries of your power that you'll encounter throughout the day," continued Amber. "It's really not that bad at all."

"I hope so," I replied.

"Last night, you mentioned that your brother goes to Brown University, why didn't he stay in San Francisco?" I asked.

"He didn't get along well with my parents. Both of us are adopted, but he never really got over it when my parents told him the truth," she said.

"Did it bother you?" I asked.

"Not really. My parents left us with our nanny most of the day because they worked. And, our nanny… well, she really didn't mind it if we went out with our friends during the week. So, I didn't really think about looking for my biological parents," Amber explained.

"Do you think that you'll ever look for them?" I asked.

"Maybe… only to figure out what to do with my powers," she continued.

"Oh! I forgot you had powers," I laughed. "You look so normal to me."

"Yeah… well, I don't have the kind of powers you will have. I guess you can say that my powers deal with the brain more than anything else," she giggled.

We arrived at the Pavilion and ordered some bagels and tea. I looked around to see who was in the room and spotted David sitting with a group of people. One of the girls, Brenda, who I knew from my Statistics class, was all over him. She was sitting next to David and constantly patting him on his shoulder. I really couldn't stand her at all.

"I don't know why she's sitting next to him," I said to Amber while looking in David's direction.

"Are you a little jealous?" she asked while sitting down at a table.

"I'm not jealous!" I said pouting. "I just don't like her…. She irritates me."

David spotted me from across the room. He left his group and quickly came over to our table. He pulled up a chair, turned it backwards, and sat on it very casually.

"Hello ladies," David said with the voice that always made me melt.

"Um…. Hi?" I said almost in shock as to how quickly he came over and placed himself next to us.

Amber ignored him.

"Katrina, we need to see each other tonight around five at the Sycamore Glen. We have to go over some things tonight," said David only looking at me and ignoring Amber because she turned her face away from him.

"Okay. Why at five?" I asked.

"I want to make sure we're alone…. See you then."

"Bye," I said. I could feel the blood rush to my cheeks as I gave him a small smile.

David got up and left. Somehow, the idea of being alone with David was starting to become more appealing to me.

He went over to talk with another group of people at an adjacent table. I couldn't make out what they were talking about, but they seemed to have a great time laughing and socializing.

"What a jerk!" yelled Amber loudly to make sure that David could hear.

David didn't even flinch.

"I don't think he's that bad Amber," I said defending David. "He hasn't done anything to me. You really need to try to be nice to him. Remember he's my partner."

Amber rolled her eyes. I ignored her.

We left breakfast and went to our general education class, *Intro to English*. I had failed the school's writing test, so I was stuck taking the class. I wasn't the most ideal student when my parent's homeschooled me. My pre-college lack of enthusiasm for the language arts was starting to show. I had to work harder than all of the other students, or, at least, that's how I felt.

I sat down in class next to Amber. Everything felt fine. I was able to feel other people's emotions as I had the other day. I also was able to read their minds. There was nothing unusual for me to think that the third phase had official started. The third phase was when I was supposed to get my powers.

The professor sat next to the podium. I wished she wouldn't have a long lecture.

"I'm so not in the mood to listen to a lecture today," I told Amber.

"I bet you're exhausted from everything that happened to you yesterday," she said.

"Yeah…. I can't wait until class is over," I said.

Professor Kramer looked up at the class and began to speak.

"Good morning class," said Professor Kramer. "I'm changing things up this morning."

"What is she talking about?" I whispered to Amber.

"I have no clue," Amber replied.

"I was thinking," said Professor Kramer as she threw her lecture notes into her folder, "today is a great day to review everything that we've learned so far."

"Take out a sheet of paper…. You need to write about your experiences in your first week at Oxy," she continued.

Was this really happening? I'm sure it was a joke. Maybe she had heard me mumble that I didn't want her to have a long lecture. And, perhaps, because of that, she was just trying to pull a gag on me.

"When you finish, leave your essay on this table…. You are dismissed after I have your essay," said Professor Kramer.

I turned and looked at Amber. I was so excited and couldn't stop smiling. Ironically, I wasn't tired anymore.

While I was writing my essay, my mind started to wander. Maybe I caused the Professor to change her lesson plan. I had to see if I was the reason for her change in plans.

I looked at Professor Kramer. She was wearing a blue long dress with open toed shoes. I thought it would be funny if she were to scratch her toes. I wanted to see if I really had the power to make her do it. The professor reached down and scratched them without stopping. I started to chuckle. Maybe I was the reason for our brief lesson plan for the day.

I started to get a slight headache, but thought it may have been from the prior day's physical transformation.

I quickly wrote my essay and left it on the table for the professor. She was still scratching her toes. I felt badly for her. I wasn't completely sure how I made her scratch her toes and tried to undo it; however, I didn't have any success in making her stop.

Despite the fact that I made the professor itch and wasn't able to reverse it, I was definitely glad I didn't have to sit through an entire lecture. Amber was still working on her essay when I left class. She was very talkative, so I could only imagine how much she could write. I didn't think she would be leaving for a while.

I walked to the quad and sat on the benches. I wanted to relax, listen to the birds chirping and smell the sweet roses. I saw David sitting with another group of people in the distance. He always seemed to have people around him.

I secretly wanted all the people around David to leave so that he would come over to hang out with me. Within moments, the crowd around David dispersed with David turning and walking away towards the opposite direction of where I sat.

I gave out a big sigh. He hadn't seen me.

There was nothing for me to do until my next class. I sat on the bench being occupied by the buzzing noises in my head. Maybe these noises were part of my second day of transformation or maybe I was in the third phase.

I started to get dizzy from the buzzing noises. They were getting louder and more intense every minute. The temples of my head kept on thumping and my ears seemed to muffle out all other noises. My heart started beating faster and faster as I fell over to my side.

"Katrina! Katrina!" yelled David as he shook me violently.

"What happened?" I said in a slurred tone. My eyes started to gradually open. I saw David holding me in my room.

"How did I get here?" I asked.

"I carried you to your room after I saw you fall on the bench. I didn't want other people to see you fall. You didn't think I was looking over at you, did you?" he continued.

"What happened to me?" I continued asking.

"You had a seizure. It's pretty common. It only means that you're starting to get your powers… your third phase," David added. "I grabbed you and ran here with light speed so that no one would see you. They wouldn't understand and you'd end up at the Health Center having a psyche evaluation."

"My headache's gone," I said more coherently as I slowly stood up off of my bed.

"Come on. Let's go to the Sycamore Glen. I think it's starting for you. We need to figure out what your powers are," said David in a rush.

He grabbed my arm, almost disregarding the fact that I had recently had a seizure and hustled me out of my room.

"Slow down," I pouted. I ripped my arm out of his tight grip.

He looked at me with his big brown eyes, smiled, and put his two hands around my waist. Within seconds, he had carried me to Sycamore Glen. I didn't know how he got me there so quickly, but I definitely knew what power he possessed.

"I was going to do this tonight, when everyone went to dinner, but we don't have much time," said David, looking around to make sure no one was at the Sycamore Glen.

"We have to grab your powers," he continued.

"What do you mean by *grab*?" I asked David.

"In order to keep a power, you need to first find out what it is. Since you had a seizure, it means that you're in the third phase…. You know, the phase that you get your powers. You have one hour to figure out all of your powers and use them intentionally at least once or else you lose them."

I started to laugh. It sounded so hilarious to me that I needed to claim my powers!

"Okay, don't believe me.... We have to figure it out! Stop laughing! We're partners and I'm definitely not going to do everything alone when we have to use our powers!" asserted David with frustration.

"Fine... tell me what I need to do and I'll listen," I said while still giggling.

David took a deep breath, relieved that I was finally going to make an effort.

"First, you need to carry me," he said. I started to laugh.

"Okay," I responded. I grabbed David and couldn't even make him move an inch.

"That's not it," mumbled David. "Run from that tree to this tree."

I jogged from one tree to another, but that wasn't good enough for David because he shook his head from side to side.

"Can you make a hole in this leaf with your eyes?" asked David as he held a leaf in his hands away from his body.

"I wish I could," I responded, disappointed that nothing seemed to be special about me.

"I give up!" exclaimed David as he threw up his arms and covered his face with his hands.

"Actually, I've had weird feelings the past two day," I told David. His eyes glowed with hope as I spoke.

"I can feel what other people feel in the room as I enter. I can hear their thoughts," I continued.

"We all can," responded David with another sigh, having given up hope once more.

"But, it's not that... something weird happened today and I don't know if it's a power. I wished that my English class teacher wouldn't have a long lecture and, sure enough, it didn't last long. Just to make sure

I wasn't going crazy, I tested it out by telepathically making her scratch her toes. She didn't stop, but I couldn't make her stop either."

"I don't know if that's a power, Katrina. It may just be a coincidence," David said with confusion. "Let's go to the quad and figure it out."

David grabbed my waist, without asking, and sped us over to the quad. It seemed to be his favorite form of transportation.

"You really need to stop that. People are going to freak out when they see you." I sounded like his mom.

"At my speed, I don't think they'd be able to see me go by," laughed David.

David smiled, ignoring my desire to have him stop using his powers in public.

I took a deep breath in and looked to see if I could control anyone. I saw Professor Kramer walking out of the building. She was still scratching her toes while carrying the essays and her notebook.

"Is that what you did to her?" asked David.

"Yeah," I said.

"That's really funny," he chuckled.

"I don't know how to make it stop," I continued.

"Well, why don't you just do the opposite of what you did?" suggested David.

"That's easier said than done," I remarked. "I guess, at this point, anything is worth trying."

I looked at her and tried to control her mind. I kept on saying in my mind, *"stop scratching your toes"*. Nothing happened.

"Why isn't it working?" I asked in a frustrated manner.

"Well, are you just thinking it or do you really want her to stop? A power doesn't work if we really don't want it to work," responded David.

"Hm… let me try it again," I said. This time I really felt my desire to make her stop scratching her toes. I could see the sparkling of my crystal belly button from my slightly raised shirt.

"It's working! It's working!" I exclaimed.

"That's awesome!" he also exclaimed.

"Wait… let me try to make her walk back inside the building," I said. I made sure I really wanted her to walk inside the building. Again, my belly button started to sparkle. I guess it was letting me know that my power is working.

Sure enough, she walked back inside the building.

"I did it!" I yelled. I started to jump up and down. I gave David a hard embrace from my excitement. I could feel his heart beating as fast as mine.

"Can you try it on someone else? I want to make sure your power works on everyone," said David.

I noticed a boy holding two books in his hands while walking next to two girls out of the Samuelson Pavilion.

"Watch! I'm going to make that boy put down his two books on the floor so that the girls next to him pick each of them off the floor," I said excitedly.

I looked at them and really concentrated. My belly button started to sparkle again. My body started to tremble in excitement and I started to giggle.

As expected, the boy put down his two books, while each girl grabbed one of his books off the floor.

I jumped up and down and even gave David another hug. He smiled.

"This is great Katrina!"

He lifted me up in the air while we both laughed in pure joy.

"There has to be something else too. You can't only have one power. We all have two. We work in twos. Two partners, two powers, get it?" he continued.

I didn't know if I even had a second set of powers. As far as I was concerned, I was happy I could control other people's thoughts.

I felt a tingling sensation in my arms. I started to get confused.

"David. My arm.... It just feels weird," I said shocked that I was getting my second power. I only had ten minutes left to figure out what my second power was or else I would lose that power forever.

"Why don't you touch something and see what happens?" suggested David.

"Okay… um… let me try this bench." I touched the bench in the quad, but nothing happened at all.

"Try something else. We don't have much time," he panted.

"Um… let me see…," I said with anxiety.

I touched the tree in the quad. As I touched it, I could see smoke starting to come out of my hands and from the tree. Everything else that I touched, didn't seem to be affected. It was only the trees that were burning from my touch. It only happened when I wanted to have them catch fire.

"Yes! That's it!" David yelled. He was more excited than me to have finally uncovered both of my powers.

"I can set trees on fire," I said perplexed.

"No... I'm sure it's much more than setting trees on fire. What else can you do with it?" asked David.

"Um... I can't shoot fire," I showed him. "But, look at this."

My hands had fire raging on top of it.

"My hands are burning, but it feels like it's a part of me," I added.

"The diamond on your neck is glowing... it must mean that you can do something with it," he said.

"I guess... I mean, if I don't know now, will I find out what it means? We only have one minute left." I was concerned.

"I hope so. If anything, you'll be able to burn trees." David gave off a roaring laugh.

"Yeah, I guess I'm a natural pyromaniac," I laughed.

"You want to grab something from the Pavilion?" he asked.

"Sure," I said excited that I was finally going to have some time to really get to know David and not all the transformation stuff that we had been talking about.

David put his hand around my shoulder as we walked toward the café. The warmth of his touch made me feel safe.

As we approached the Samuelson Pavilion, I heard a group of sorority girls. One of them came over and grabbed David's hand off my shoulder. She completely ignored my presence and pulled him away from me. Ugh! It was Brenda!

"Hi... David," said Brenda with a flirtatious grin.

"Hi, Brenda," said David.

"Want to come to our party later? It starts at eight. You can bring Karen with you." Brenda snickered as she called me Karen.

"You mean, Katrina," I quickly responded.

"Um... Kat... whatever," said Brenda as she grabbed David's arm and yanked him towards her.

"Come on, you've got to stop this!" exclaimed David. "I'll be at the party only if Katrina comes with me." He turned around and winked to keep the peace.

"Sure," I said confused. Brenda threw me a dirty look. I think she expected me not to go to the party.

"Hey! We're heading inside. Do you want to get something small to eat?" asked Brenda while looking directly at David. "She can join us too. What'd you say, Katty?"

"Actually, I've lost my appetite," I responded.

I got irritated and left in a fury. I could hear David in the distance calling out to me.

"Katrina! Come back! They're just kidding!" he shouted.

I turned and looked at him. He was standing alone, while the sorority girls were already walking into the Pavilion.

I didn't need to put up with Brenda's insults. She didn't even have the decency to remember my name or make any effort to be nice. I wanted to find

Amber and just vent.

CHAPTER FIVE

It was eight o'clock and I was determined to go to the sorority party despite Brenda's insults. After all, I was invited and needed to make sure Brenda didn't sink her claws into David.

I had convinced Amber to go with me. She was always willing to go to any social function. I, on the other hand, was simply going to make sure that David and Brenda wouldn't become an item.

I looked at myself in the mirror and still couldn't get over how beautiful my golden hair looked. I put on some make up, which was rare for me. I also wore some higher heeled boots to complement my skin tight acid washed jeans. I wore a fitted dark colored shirt so that my golden hair would stand out for David, who I definitely wanted to notice me.

Amber knocked on my door.

"Are you ready?" she asked.

"Yeah! Let's go!" I said quickly.

My stomach was churning from nervousness. This was my first party at school. I wasn't even cordially invited to this one. Brenda had invited me begrudgingly, so it made me much more nervous to be at the party.

"We have to stop by David's dorm," I told Amber. David lived in Bell Young, which was only thirty feet away from Wylie Hall, where I lived.

"We don't have to…. We can go alone," Amber said without any desire to see him.

"I don't think we would have been invited if David wasn't with me this morning," I said.

"And… you wanted to be invited?" she asked.

"No, but I don't want Brenda to claw her way into David either," I replied.

I still couldn't figure out why Amber didn't like him. Something must have happened during the second phase of my transformation in my room. I was going to ignore it for now. I had to focus on going to the party and not fainting from my nervousness.

David was in front of the dorm waiting for us.

"Ready to have some fun!" David exclaimed while rubbing his hands together.

"Yeah. I can't wait to see Brenda," I said with a smirk on my face.

"She's not that bad, you know. You really need to lighten up," said David.

"Lighten up! I'm as light as a feather," I said sarcastically.

"Katrina, your problem is that you don't give people a chance," continued David.

David was now acting like he was some sort of therapist. I know who I like and who I don't like. If Brenda belittles me, then I think it's fair to say that she's not on my favorites list.

Amber stayed quiet, which was very unusual. She was not happy David was with us, so I didn't want to ask her what was wrong. It was a really quiet walk to the sorority house.

When we arrived, there were large groups of people crowding the lawn and the inside of the house. The music was playing so loudly that it hurt my ears.

There were people socializing and dancing everywhere in the house. The sorority had hired a DJ who was playing the music outside. There was a lot of laughter and the crowds near the DJ seemed to get larger by the minute.

"Want to dance?" asked David.

"Sure," I said. "Come on Amber."

I grabbed Amber's hand and started to dance with David. Within minutes, I noticed that David had disappeared.

"Did you see David?" I asked Amber.

"No. He was dancing with us a minute ago," she said.

"I guess he'll turn up," I said worried that Brenda was the cause of David's disappearance.

"Forget about him. Let's keep dancing," Amber said.

I started to dance, feeling the thrill of the moment. I had completely forgotten about Brenda and David.

Amber threw her hands in the air and started to jump while dancing. Everyone on the dance floor seemed to be dancing in unison. We were all dancing together. No one was left to dance alone. I was so happy. I couldn't stop smiling. Seconds became minutes and minutes became hours while we continued to dance continuously and breathlessly, without any moment to care about anything.

Everything changed when I spotted Brenda on the dance floor with David. I cringed. David seemed to enjoy being around Brenda. He didn't even bother to look at me and Amber. Brenda made eye contact with me. I heard Brenda saying to herself, *"Ha! Ha! You're not even good enough for him. No competition."*

I was so upset. I wish I couldn't read her mind. I had to do something! I used my newly acquired power to make her like me. The look on Brenda's face changed from her squinting evil eyes to a pleasant smile. I could see the crystal on my belly button illuminate as I used my power. Brenda started walking towards me with David following her.

"Hi, Katrina!" shouted Brenda. "I'm so glad you came!"

"Yeah! It's great to see you again," I said, secretly happy that I was able to use my powers to my advantage.

I know it was terrible of me to change Brenda's perception of me, but it made me feel so much better. I was tired of her snickering remarks. She wanted to belittle me any chance she got and I was now able to change the way she acted towards me.

As I stood there with my glory, I noticed a black cloud fade over the lighting in the room. It came and went numerous times. I thought it was a series of power outages. I started to feel dizzy. The dark cloud rapidly took over and I fainted. I don't remember what happened. I only remember waking up in my bed with Amber and David watching over me.

"What happened?" I asked David and Amber.

"You used your powers! That's what happened," said David furiously.

"What's wrong with that?" I asserted.

"You can't use your powers until you're fully transformed," said Amber. "I'm glad you only fainted. You could have fallen into a coma and then we would have had to call our Council."

"There's a Council?" I asked. I never knew there were a lot of us *special* people in the world. Imagine having enough for a Council. That would mean that we have our own society.

"Yes," responded Amber. "The Council lives in the caldera of Mammoth Mountain... here in California. They're responsible for all of us."

"We have to follow the rules Katrina!" David said furiously.

"The Council makes sure that we don't misuse our powers. If we do, they strip us of our powers," continued Amber.

"Yeah, and the rule states that you can't use your powers during the final phase of your transformation, other than to see if it works. Obviously, you used it at the party."

"I didn't know I would end up fainting," I said justifying my actions.

"I'm glad you woke up," said Amber relieved.

"We could have gotten into trouble!" exclaimed David. "Both of us could have had one power stripped from each one of us. We're so lucky you woke up. Otherwise, we would have to drive you to the Council."

"We're responsible for you Karina," added David. "Until, you complete your transformation, Amber and I are supposed to make sure everything goes as planned."

"I never asked to be whatever I am!" I yelled. "I never knew using my power was a problem. It would've been nice if you told me."

I was upset because there were rules that no one ever told me about. I didn't even know that there was a Council. If David and Amber had told me, I wouldn't have put myself in such a bad situation.

"Anyway, we're glad we don't have to report anything back to the Council," said Amber trying to calm down David. David huffed and turned his back away from me.

"We have to take you to the Council today," continued Amber.

"What? Are you going to tell them about what I did last night?" I asked confused.

"No," Amber responded with the longest 'no' I had ever heard. "We have to take you to the Council because you need to complete your final phase of transformation. Usually, the Council meets every Saturday, but during transformations, they make exception and meet other days too. I'm glad it's a Sunday so that we don't have to worry about school," continued Amber.

"We have to leave," said David after finally turning back to look at me. "It's going to be a long drive, probably five to six hours."

We grabbed a few bagels from the Samuelson Pavilion and decided to drive out to Mammoth. I offered to drive, but David had a car too and he had driven out there before. Besides, neither David nor Amber wanted me to drive after my fainting incident. David ended up driving.

CHAPTER SIX

It was a long drive out to the Long Valley Caldera in Mammoth. David didn't speak to me at all during the drive. He was still upset about how I used my powers to manipulate Brenda, which almost cost him his powers.

Amber, on the other hand, wouldn't stop talking. She talked about anything and everything. She spoke about the people in her classes and who she liked or disliked. The topics of conversation were endless for Amber. I tuned her out and stared into the emptiness of the Mojave Desert.

The trip seemed endless and, at times, annoying because David wouldn't say a word and Amber wouldn't stop talking.

We finally reached the Hot Springs in the Long Valley Caldera.

"This is it. We have to walk the rest of the way," said David.

"I don't see anything. Only rocks," I said.

"It's up the rocky path. You can't miss the Hot Springs after your hike up there," he added.

"What? You're not coming?" I asked.

"Huh... Maybe I should stay back in the car," he replied. His voice made it clear that he was still not happy with me.

I got out of the car and slammed the door shut. I was starting to get really frustrated because he was making it clear with his voice intonation that he was still upset. I needed to put an end to his poutiness towards me.

"David, you need to stop being so mean to me! We're partners, right?" I said forcefully, hoping that it would make everything go back to the way it was. I saw Amber slowly moving away from us to find a rock to sit on.

David stopped and looked at me with a deep and torturous stare.

"What do you think?" questioned David. The tone of his voice that once made my heart melt, resonated with his dismay in my actions.

"Of course, we're partners. That doesn't stop the fact that you almost killed yourself! You also could have gotten one of our powers taken away," continued David, as he pointed to himself and Amber. Amber shied away, trying to stay out of the argument.

"I'm sorry, but you should have told me!" I exclaimed. "Unlike you and Amber, who had people guiding you through this process, I don't have anyone."

I started to cry. I felt all alone, even though Amber and David were supposed to be like me.

David took his hand and put it on my shoulder. His facial appearance changed from anger to sorrow.

"No, I'm sorry," said David in a low voice. "You're my partner and we have to work together like a team. I should have told you. I didn't know you would try to use your powers!"

I looked up at him and saw the sincerity in his facial expressions. I cleared the tears off my face with the back of my hands and nodded my head to accept his apology.

"I wasn't happy that we went to the party together and Brenda just snatched you away from us," I said to justify my actions.

"She didn't snatch me away…. She… she…," tried to explain David.

"She, what?" I asked.

"Come on…. Let's go!" yelled Amber in the distance.

I never got my answer.

"We have to follow the red rocks to the Hot Springs," added Amber as she walked up the gently sloping hill.

The walk to the Hot Springs was long and arduous. I wish our car was able to go over the rocky road. David didn't want to risk getting a flat tire. I didn't understand why. I'm sure he could have carried us back to school faster than if we were taking a drive in his car.

We finally reached the Hot Springs. There were pools of water with steam coming from them.

"It's this way," David said as he directed us towards the hot springs' pool inside a cave.

"Come on Katrina!" yelled Amber.

"I can't help looking at the bubbling water. I've never seen anything like this before," I explained to David and Amber with awe.

"Don't you know that we're standing over a volcano?" asked Amber.

"Really? I never thought about it," I replied. I remember from my homeschooled science class that calderas are areas of land over a volcano. They form a crater-like valley after a volcanic eruption has made the volcano's mountain fall down. I now understood why the pools of water were now boiling. The Long Valley Caldera was very large. I never thought there would still be an active volcano underneath this caldera.

We reached a special red rock inside the cave. David gently touched the rock and it opened. As he was touching the red rock, I noticed that the golden star on his neck was glowing. He turned and smiled at me, realizing that I had discovered why the red rock moved when he touched it.

I carefully stepped into the passageway. It was dark and rocky. We could only see a red glow at the end of the passageway. As I stepped out of the passageway and into the larger area of the cave, my eyes could not stop gazing at the sight of the beautiful red crystals all over the walls of the cave. Each crystal was stacked next to another one, without leaving any room in between them. Even the ceilings had red crystals affixed to the walls of the cave.

"Follow me," said David.

"Where are we going?" I asked.

"I'll show you," responded David.

"Don't worry Katrina. I'm pretty sure David has been here many times. I haven't been here since I first transformed. Usually, you don't need to meet with the Council, but David is an exception to the rule," Amber snickered as she spoke.

I followed David's lead into another passageway inside the illuminating cave.

CHAPTER SEVEN

The passageway led us to a very different room. The new room in the cave had an orange glow to it. The transparent floor showed the red lava quickly moving around in the volcano. The room was covered with golden stars. In the middle of the room hung a very large diamond star, which measured about two feet in size.

"I can't go in there," said Amber.

"Why not?" I asked.

"I won't be able to walk on the protective floor that you can walk over," she replied. "I'm not chosen."

"I don't understand what you mean," I asked perplexed about the word *chosen*.

"I just can't!" insisted Amber as she pushed me to go over to David.

I was afraid that I would fall through too.

"Katrina, you'll be fine," insisted David as he stood over the transparent floor. He reached out his hand so that I wouldn't feel like I would fall through.

I carefully placed my feet on the transparent flooring while holding David's hand, thinking that I would be the one falling down into the lava.

"I can't believe it! I didn't fall!" I exclaimed.

I looked down at the lava and was amazed that I was standing directly above it. I had a huge grin over my face as I realized how extraordinary this really was.

"Amber, come on over.... Look! I'm standing on the floor too," I said as I jumped up on the transparent floor.

"Sorry.... I'm not allowed to be in there," said Amber.

"Katrina... don't go back to Amber... this is the Sancdia. The Sancdia is a sacred room that we, the Protectins, can only enter," said David as he moved me away from Amber.

Just as David finished speaking, the passage way door shut. David and I were alone in the room with the golden star walls.

Another door opened. Slowly, the ten Council members stepped out in pairs. They were not old, contrary to what I had thought. They were as young as me, which was very surprising. The Council members wore golden hooded capes that were outlined by silver and red strips of silk.

The Council formed a circle around me and David and bowed down to us. I was shocked.

David stood directly in front of me.

"Hold my hands," said David with his overpowering voice as he reached out both hands to me. His voice was so persuasive and charismatic that I naturally listened to him.

"David, what's happening?" I asked.

Within minutes, I felt dizzy. I started to see golden stars flying in the air. The lava below me seemed like it had encircled me and David. I saw David's eyes glowing as he stared directly into mine. I looked at my hands and they were glowing too. I looked golden and, when I looked at David, he looked golden too. My heart raced and then everything turned black.

"Katrina! It's over!" exclaimed David.

The Council was still surrounding us, bowing down as we had left them. Our skin color was no longer golden. However, we had golden hooded capes with diamond stars all over them.

"Amber wanted me to tell you what was going to happen, but I didn't want to," said David.

"She thinks I'm a jerk for not letting you know what I am about to tell you," he continued.

"You see... we're the leaders of the Council. You and I were chosen at birth to lead our people. The large size of the golden star behind your neck represents our position. Your father and my mother were the leaders of the Council. Since the Mutineers rose up against our kind and kidnapped your father, you and I are now left to lead the Council," added David.

I was shocked that my father had not died. Why did my mother lie to me about my father's death? All this time, I thought he had a heart attack and that I would never see him again. I felt sad inside. Everything that made sense to me was, once again, torn apart. I desperately wanted to leave to speak to my mother.

"My father's still alive?" I asked trying to make sure that David was not making anything up.

"Yes, but we don't know where he's at. The Mutineers took him and want to transform him so that they can have access to the diamond star," continued David.

"So, they want it because they're greedy?" I asked.

"Partly... the diamond controls the volcanic activity in the world. I will let the Council explain. Council, please rise," commanded David.

The Council in unison said, "Yes, Superior."

They bowed after standing.

One of the Council members began to speak. She was the Council member in charge of knowledge.

"The Mutineers have red stars on their necks. They were once our kind and were actually Council members. However, they were corrupted after one of them became too greedy in the world. In fact, it was Tibeno, your mother's partner," she stated.

"Tibeno was upset that your father, who was the leader, was in a relationship with your mother. Out of jealousy, Tibeno convinced a few members of our Council to overthrow your father's power. He also wanted to control the volcanoes to make more money. Your father found out through David's mother who was approached by Tibeno," continued the Council member in charge of technology.

"David's mother and your father then banished Tibeno and the other rogue members of the Council. When they were stripping Tibeno of his powers, he managed to escape with a few others. Their golden stars turned red, signifying their Mutineer status in our society," said another Council member in charge of diplomacy.

"This means that they weren't fully banished," finalized the Council member in charge of knowledge.

"I don't understand why it would be a problem if Tibeno's not banished. I mean, how could controlling the volcano make him rich?" I asked out of curiosity.

"Each volcano has a large forty carat star diamond. If the diamond is removed, the volcano will have an explosive eruption that will kill millions of people within five cities around the volcano. The Long Valley Caldera is the main volcano. A removal of the diamond here can trigger earthquakes all over the world. It's not a normal eruption. This eruption will cause massive devastation. Until a new diamond is created by the volcano, the earthquakes won't stop," said the Council member in charge of technology.

"This is unreal!" I exclaimed.

"If you don't believe them, just look over here," said David as he took my hand and guided me to the magnificent diamond. It was hidden behind a lava rock full of colorful gems. The glow was spectacular.

"I don't know what to say... I've never seen anything like this before," I said while gazing at the diamond that was so clear in color that it sparkled effortlessly.

"We can't let anyone remove this diamond. We have to protect it," said David. "If Tibeno gets a hold of it, it's all over for us."

"David's right. Obviously, the diamond itself will make Tibeno rich, but so many lives will be lost because of it. The removal of the diamond will shift the world's balance. Once the diamond is removed for a full day, Tibeno will be able to control all of the diamonds. He will become a Council leader and can use it for his own greed," said the Council member in charge of knowledge.

"But, isn't Tibeno at least partly banished?" I asked.

"Yeah, but your dad isn't. Only the Council members and the leaders can step on the transparent floors. Everyone else will fall into the lava," said David. "But, your dad is still technically the leader of the Council. Tibeno can use him to have access to the Sancdia."

"My dad won't let anyone control him," I insisted.

"If they find a way transform your father to follow their lead, he won't have a choice. He's still able to step on the transparent floor and he hasn't been stripped from his powers. Tibeno knows what he's doing and we have to find him both your dad and Tibeno," said David.

"I just don't get it. Why didn't my mom tell me all of this? Why did they lie to me all these year? You know, I spent most of my childhood away from people. I didn't know it was because they were hiding something from me," I said sadly.

"Your father was forced to live in the mountains because the Mutineers were going to take you and your father away. If they succeeded, the Mutineers could have already taken over the world. I was in the same situation as you. My mom had us live far away from everyone too. Both of our parents did it to protect the future of our people," said David, trying to calm me down.

All of this information was overwhelming. I slowly fell onto my knees. I wanted to roll up like a ball and disappear.

"Katrina, I know this is overwhelming and that's why Amber is mad at me. She wanted me to tell you slowly and not just spring it on you like this," said David with a comforting voice.

"This is too much for me to handle!" I exclaimed. I looked at David. His golden hair blended in perfectly with the walls in the room.

"It's okay, Katrina. We'll get through this," David tried to comfort me again. "We need to work together to find your father."

"David, you don't understand. I could have had a normal childhood. I didn't need to be homeschooled. Robbie was the only friend I had growing up. I didn't know anyone else. That's not normal! I was living in a box," I broke down in tears.

"I'm sorry... but, you can't give up on me. We have to work together. We need to find your father now so that we can take away his powers and let him retire to a normal life. If he is retired, he will not be able to enter the room with the diamond," said David.

"We are the Protectins, Katrina. We are the guardians of the volcanic diamonds," continued David. "You and I were chosen to lead the Protectins and to make sure that there isn't anyone that's trying to shift the balance. We can't let what happened to Tibeno occur again."

David had finally convinced me not to feel helpless. His charismatic voice had overcome my doubts and fears. His voice had overpowered me as it had when we had first met. David had managed to persuade me now when I felt the most vulnerable.

"If we are the Protectins.... I guess, the protectors of the volcanic diamonds, who are people like Amber?" I asked.

"Amber is a Minder. She helps the Protectins by informing us if there are any threats to the diamond stars. In essence, she's like a spy by telling us what she knows. She also helps protect us from any threats to our lives," explained David.

"She's not allowed in this room?" I continued asking.

"No, only the members of the Council are allowed in this room… and the only people who are able to touch the diamond stars without having their powers taken away are the Council leaders, which are you and me. Your father and my mother are also Council leaders. However, when I found you, I was forced to have my mother return to a normal life so that we could lead the Council. Everything is done in pairs and her partner, your father, is now missing," said David.

I had finally realized that this was now my destiny. I was a Protectin, the guardian of the volcanic diamonds. Not an ordinary Protectin, but one of the leaders of the Protectins. My life of living in the shadows by being sheltered from the world was only done to protect my future. It was now time for me to break out of my shell and act like a true leader.

CHAPTER EIGHT

When we returned from the Long Valley Caldera in Mammoth, I was so exhausted both mentally and physically. I kept on trying out my new powers in private so that I would learn to use them better. I set a small bush on fire, but quickly put it out with a bottle of water. Although I loved going to Professor Smith's class, I managed to have him give us a day off from reading in our Politics textbook with my telepathic powers.

It was hard for me to act like nothing had changed in my life. I realized that I had transformed into the leader of the Protectins. More importantly, I knew that my father was alive. I had to figure out a way to get him back safely. I had to figure out a plan before speaking to David. I decided that I would drive out to Topanga after my morning classes to talk to my mother. Amber volunteered to go with me on my midweek excursion. I don't think David even noticed because Brenda was keeping him pretty occupied with all of her sorority events.

Amber and I sat in my car.

"I'm so excited to meet your mom!" Amber said loudly.

"She's really nice," I said very briefly while only thinking about Tibeno and how he had kidnapped my father.

"Amber, what does a Minder do?" I asked, just getting to the point.

"I don't know too much about what we do," responded Amber. "All I know is that once I find my partner, we will be able to work together to find out information for the Protectins. I guess you can call us spies for the Protectins."

"How many of you are there?" I continued asking.

"Well, there are about 1,500 volcanoes that are somewhat active on land and each volcano has twenty Minders to support the needs of the ten Protectins. The Mammoth Mountain volcano is the main volcano, so there are two additional Protectins which are you two. If anything happens to that volcano, all volcanoes will erupt. That's why you and David went there. You are the leader of all of us, not only the Protectins. You are at the top of our hierarchy," explained Amber.

"So, if I ask you to find out information for me, will you?" I continued asking.

"Yes, only if it is something that you and David mutually want to find out. Obviously, if it's not too important, I would always find out for you, despite the rules," she responded while she winked at me.

"Have you tried out any of your power?" I asked.

"Yeah, but I'm not so good at it yet. My parents aren't Minders because, you know, I'm adopted. They had me try to figure things out myself," she said.

"So, you didn't have anyone to help you through the process also?" I asked.

"No. But, I didn't feel your pain in the transformation. My parents made sure I didn't have any pain," she smiled.

"Lucky. I think that was the worst part," I replied.

"As far as the Minder powers, I kind of learned everything as I went along. Sometimes, I look straight and I see a holographic computer screen in front of me. It's weird seeing words and numbers when I talk to my friends," she explained.

"I can't imagine how you could focus," I said.

"It took some time. The one thing that I know for sure is that I can communicate to whichever Protectin I want to by switching to them on my holographic screen. My parents told me about that and I tried it out with them. It took a few tries, but I think I've got it down to a science now," she added.

"Do you have any physical powers?" I asked.

"No," she said.

"Ha! Ha! Ha! I guess we're the ones that fight, huh?" I said laughing.

"Yeah... that's one way of looking at it," she said.

Time went by quickly as I asked Amber the details of her job. She was basically the Protectins' informant. She would get us answers whenever we needed to know something. Her powers were physical, but rather mental. She could read the minds of people. She also had the capability to use technology beyond the means of any government organization to find out information. She was like a mini-government agency for the Protectins. Unfortunately, she hadn't found her partner yet, so she was not able to fully explore her skills.

When I was in the City of Topanga, Amber insisted that we stop off at an artistic store that sold sculptures. She said that she's always loved brass sculptures and was hoping to find a small one for her dorm room.

We stopped off at Jack's Unique Collections. The store looked like an old wooden home with all of the sculptures displayed outside in the front of the house. There was a chain link fence to separate the store from the road. Adjacent to the fence was a private area for parking.

I parked my car and was eager to see what sculptures Jack had displayed. Sometimes, my mom and dad would sell their artwork there on consignment. Jack would let them sell the sculptures in return for a portion of the sale. My parents had a number of places that they would sell their artwork for a living. I wondered if my mother had recently dropped off any of her artwork for Jack to sell.

"Oh, hello Katrina!" exclaimed Jack as he came to embrace me. "It's been such a long time since I last saw you."

"Hi, Jack," I replied.

Jack was in his mid-forties. His dark black hair was just below his shoulders. Jack had a beautiful dark glow to his skin that radiated as he walked over in his orange colored shirt. He had a son that I would play with every time my parents brought me to his store. There were really only a handful of kids that I ever saw growing up and Robert, or Robbie, was one of them.

"Is Robbie here?" I asked.

"Yes, he's inside the store polishing a brass sculpture that just came in. I'm sure he will be excited to see you. Who is this young lady with you?" asked Jack in a fatherly manner.

"It's my friend Amber. I met Amber on my first day at Oxy and we've been best friends since then!" I said excitedly.

It's so nice to actually say that I have a best friend. After having grown up mostly by myself, saying that I had a friend, let alone a best friend, made me feel ecstatic.

"Hello, Amber. My name is Jack. I've known Katrina since she was very young. She's really a great young lady. Excuse me for a moment. I want to get my son Robbie out here to see Katrina. He hasn't seen her for several months," Jack said as he looked at Amber.

He then continued, "Robbie drove home from UCLA last night. He's going back tomorrow for classes. I'm sure he will love to see you Katrina." Jack looked at me with a big smile on his face.

Amber looked around at the beautiful sculptures.

"Wow, these are absolutely gorgeous, but too pricey for me to buy," said Amber as she looked at the prices of each sculpture.

"My mom made this one Amber," I said.

It was a bronze sculpture of a girl sitting next to a tree with her hands over her sad face encircled by a tear drop.

"She made it after I lost my dad to what I thought was a heart attack," I said as I sighed and snickered at the same time, realizing that my mom had lied to me about my dad's condition. I still couldn't believe that she told me he was dead when in fact he was kidnapped.

"It's amazing how she captured your feelings of hurt," said Amber, sounding like an art critic.

Robbie walked out of the store eager to see me.

"Katrina, I've missed you!" exclaimed Robbie.

Robbie had dark brown hair and beautiful blue eyes. He embraced me so tightly that I thought my bones were about to break. I don't know if I'm sensitive to touch, but it was as strong as when David had hugged me tightly in the quad after I had discovered my powers.

"I've missed you too," I said as I continued to hug Robbie.

"You've changed so much," he said.

"Really, it's not like I've done anything special," I replied.

"Maybe I'm just used to seeing you hiking with me in the hills," Robbie responded.

"What? I'm not always dirty! I know you've seen me without dirt on my clothes," I said laughing.

"Yeah," said Robbie in a daze, "but there's something different about you and I just can't figure it out.

Robbie then turned and looked at Amber. He quickly let me go and fell into a trance.

"Hi... I'm Robbie," said Robbie staring directly into Amber's beautiful blue eyes.

Their eyes looked identical.

"Hi... I'm Amber," said Amber really slowly.

They extended their hands slowly to greet each other. They looked directly into each other's eyes. There was no movement other than a gentle touch of each other's hands. I felt like I was out of place. Robbie and Amber seemed to have forgotten that I even existed. They just stared at each other. I could see shiny tear drops falling out of Amber's crystal-like blue eyes.

As I turned and looked at Robbie, I noticed that he had a blue crystal starting to form on his neck. I realized that Robbie and Amber had found each other. It was Robbie's turn to transform. I didn't know how to feel about the situation. I felt excited for Amber because she had found Robbie. On the other hand, I was so miserable inside because I knew the kind of pain that Robbie would have to undergo to transform into a Minder.

I put my hands on my head and started to panic. Why was I panicking? I'm a leader of the Protectins, right? I'm strong, right? Maybe, I'm not fit to be a leader?

Jack ran over to me and grabbed me by both of my shoulders. I think he thought I was about to fall.

"Katrina, it's okay. It's Robbie's turn now. Don't worry. I will make sure he has an easy transformation," reassured Jack as he saw that I was about to cry.

He slowly let go of me after realizing that my initial shock had slowly worn off.

"We all have feelings," continued Jack. "Even leaders of the Protectins have emotions. After all, we are just a different breed of humans. We still have the same emotions even though we may have a special purpose."

"What? How do you know that?" I asked.

How did Jack know I was the leader of the Protectins? Do I look that different?

"I'm a Minder, Katrina," continued Jack. "I knew you were Kevin's successor."

I hadn't noticed Jack's blue diamond on his neck because it was hidden behind his hair. Jack pulled his hair back to prove his Minder status in our society.

"Lorina told me that Kevin is missing," said Jack. "I don't know where he's at. I've tapped into all my resources and I don't know what else to do."

Robbie and Amber had not moved. They held each other's hands with a deep stare into each other's eyes. It looked like that moment had not ended and his pain had not started.

Jack seemed to completely disregard the fact that his son was about to be in agony within moments of him speaking to me. He was more interested in my needs rather than his son's transformation.

"Don't you care?" I blurted out.

"Of course, I care about Kevin!" said Jack, misunderstanding that I meant my father rather than his son, Robbie.

"No!" I shouted. "I mean, don't you care that your son is going to experience the worse pain ever imagined within just minutes of us talking here?"

I was furious. I had known Robbie since I could remember and wouldn't want to wish all the agony I felt onto anyone.

Jack started to laugh.

"Poor Katrina!" giggled Jack, "We have ways to avoid the pain. There is a powder that I will sprinkle on him when the pain begins which will stop his pain within thirty minutes. He will only feel a little bit of discomfort. You must have transformed away from home."

Jack put his left hand on his face and swayed his head gently from left to right, looking like he felt sorry for me.

Great! Of all people, I had to be the one that had to transform the hard way!

"Amber," I said trying to ruin their moment. "Amber… Amber!"

"Um… huh," said Amber, coming out of a trance.

"I want to go see my mom," I said, peeved that I had transformed the hard way and didn't have anyone to help me other than David and Amber who babysat me through the process. I'm glad that they were around me because I think I wouldn't have made it through my transformation without them. No wonder they told me that it's easier when you transform at home. All I hoped for now is that no one else felt the agony that I did.

"Amber," I continued saying. Amber did not seem to get out of her trance completely.

"Just go home Katrina. You can pick me up on your way back," said Amber very slowly.

"Don't worry," added Jack, "Remember how you felt the first time you met David? Well, this is the same thing."

"How do you know about David?" I asked feeling my privacy had been completely violated.

"We all know about you and David, Katrina. We're Minders and our job is to make sure that we have as much information as possible for our leaders. The Minders have been monitoring you and David since you were born. There have been people around you watching to see when you would transform. You are our leaders now. It's our job to make sure that nothing happened to you during your transformation and that you did get all of your powers. We wouldn't want a leader without powers, right?" Jack chuckled.

It all started making sense.

"Oh... okay. Well, I guess, I will pick up Amber in a few hours," I said.

"Sure. I'll let her know…. I need to teach them both their roles since they have finally found each other. Amber and Robbie will report directly to you and David. All other Minders will need to report to them," indicated Jack.

I was very excited that my best friend was going to be one of the most powerful people in the Minder's hierarchy.

CHAPTER NINE

When I drove up to our house, my mom had the garage door open. She was painting the mountainous scenery in front of her. I quickly came out of the car and gave her a big hug.

"I missed you!" I squealed.

"Me too sweetie," said my mom as if I were a child in grade school.

"I'm so happy that you transformed," continued my mom. "With your dad missing, I wasn't sure what was going to happen to the volcanic diamonds. I'm worried that Tibeno may have your dad."

My mom did not wait to make small talk. She just went straight to the point. It seemed like she had been worried about Tibeno and my dad for a while and needed to get it off her chest.

"My transformation was really bad," I said bluntly while trying to get her sympathy.

"I'm sorry to hear that….," she said as she gave me a hug. "Sometimes, things happen that we never expect. It just makes us stronger. It makes YOU stronger."

She put her hand on my shoulder and guided me into the house.

"There are more pressing things that we need to discuss," said my mom.

We walked inside the house. My mom had a beautifully carved wooden box sitting in the middle of the coffee table. It wasn't painted, nor did it look varnished. It had a very detailed carving of a star in the middle of the box. When she opened the box, I saw a golden necklace with a diamond star pendant.

"Your dad had told me to give this to you whenever you get your powers," said Mom.

Just as my mom finished speaking, her cell phone rang.

"Hello... yes... oh... hi... she is... sure... right now... talk to you soon! Bye!" my mom said as she hung up her phone.

"Who was that?" I asked.

"Oh… it was David's mom. She's a really nice lady. I'm glad she was your dad's partner," Mom responded. "Here, why don't you wear the necklace?"

My mom delicately removed the necklace from the box. The diamond star glowed even more brightly outside of the box. She placed the necklace over my head.

Instantly, I felt my body tingle and slowly fade away. I felt a whirl of wind surround my body as if I were in a tornado. Within moments, I felt like I was floating in the sky surrounded by the cool winds of the tornado that encircled me. My body continued to tingle in pulses that only magnified as I felt like I was floating higher in the sky. I didn't know where I was and where I was going. All I could see were the leaves that had gathered from the rapid wind that was encircling me.

Slowly, my tingling sensation began to fade. The wind began to slow down. I felt my feet touch the ground. Then, all the leaves that once flew passionately around me, dropped to the floor faster than I had time to blink.

I looked around me. I saw David in front of me with a necklace that had a diamond star around his neck as well. We were at the Sycamore Glen. However, this time, we were not out in the open. There was a golden-red shield that had encased us inside the quaint woodsy area of our school.

"David, do you know what's going on?" I asked with confusion while walking towards him.

"No, my mom put this necklace on me and here I am," he replied.

"They probably planned it," I said. "That's why your mom called my mom."

After I spoke, the Council that I had met at Mammoth's volcano appeared in the same tornado clouds that had brought me and David to the Sycamore Glen. Once again, they encircled David and me and bowed down in respect.

One of the members of the Council rose.

"As the Protectin of Continuity, I have set up a couple of challenges for you to help you strengthen your abilities. Unfortunately, if you do not pass these challenges, you will be asked to step down from your status as leaders of our people and protectors of the volcanic diamonds. The shield around the Sycamore Glen will prevent outsiders from observing our challenges. Use your powers wisely and as a pair," said the Protectin of Continuity.

I had heard pair and partner so many times, almost too many times.

I wanted the challenges to be over. I took a deep sigh and looked into David's eyes. His golden hair glistened even more intensely in the enclosed area. I looked down at my curly golden highlighted hair and saw that each piece looked like real strands of gold.

"We've got this," David said confidently.

"I hope so," I replied.

"Hey… don't worry. If our parents went through this and made it, I'm sure it's nothing," he responded. I was hoping David was right.

110

The Council quickly stood up and disappeared in the same type of tornados that had brought them to the Sycamore Glen. The first event in our challenge quickly followed upon their departure.

A group of five screaming children with lizard faces appeared from underneath the park table. At first, they seemed harmless. However, as the minutes went by, their screams became louder and louder. It was unbearable.

David tried to push them under the table, but they were as strong as him. He was not getting anywhere with his powers.

I set a small branch on fire and waved it at the lizard-children. They didn't seem to care as they continued screaming louder and louder. As each moment passed, the screams magnified.

"David!" I screamed.

It was so loud that I could only see David mouth the words 'what' to me. The screams had become so loud that my skin began to wrinkle in different directions with each scream.

I remembered that David and I can communicate telepathically. I closed my eyes and started to speak to David with my thoughts.

"David, can you hear me?" I asked David, hoping that we were still able to communicate telepathically.

"Yeah. I can hear you," he responded back telepathically.

"There has to be a way to stop this screaming," I said.

The screaming had become so intense that we felt a gust of wind every time a lizard-child screamed. Both of our skins pulled back even further into their newly accustomed wrinkly positions.

"We need to calm them down," said David telepathically.

"Hm...," I responded. *"Maybe if I sing them a lullaby while controlling their minds, it may soothe them."*

"I'll carry each one to the table area so that they can crawl back under the table," continued David with our plan.

I looked at all the lizard-children and tried to control their minds. I tried to remember how I had done it with my professors. The noise of the screams was overbearing. I took a few deep breaths and tried to concentrate.

I started to sing a lullaby that my mom sang to me when I was a little girl.

"It's time to sleep,
Your time to sleep,
Slowly close your eyes.

It's time to dream,
Your time to dream,
Let go of those cries.

Sleep a little,
Dream a little,
Bring your fantasies alive.

It's time to sleep,
This time you'll sleep,
No need to say good night."

The screams started to get lower and lower. Finally, each one of the lizard-children had stopped screaming.

David carried one over to the park table, but it started to scream again. He scratched his head and thought.

"Why is it crying again? I didn't do anything wrong," he said telepathically.

"You need to be quicker," I replied. I resumed singing and was able to calm down the newly screaming child that David had brought to the park table. Finally, it stopped crying.

"Quick! Put it under the table!" I said quickly.

"I've got it," he replied.

David put the lizard-child under the table. It came back out, but did not make any noise.

"It stopped crying! But, I don't know why it's not going under the table," said David perplexed.

"I don't know, but as long as it's not screaming, just go get the others," I replied

telepathically. There was no use in speaking. The noises of the lizard-children were still overpowering.

David then carried the second lizard-child to the park table. However, this time, he used his speed to carry the child within ten feet of where it originally stood. The lizard-child did not cry or seem to have noticed that it was carried back to the table. Once all five lizard-children were next to the table, they slowly went under the table and disappeared.

I enjoyed the moment of silence and only wondered what challenge would be next.

There were ten dots descending quickly down the golden skylight of the enclosed Sycamore Glen.

"What is that?" I asked terrified.

"They're hawks! They're the biggest hawks I've ever seen!" yelled David.

Each hawk had a ten feet wide wingspan. They were black with red piercing eyes and had gray feathers drooping down their bodies as they flew in the air.

"They're heading straight towards us!" I yelled.

"Hurry! Let's get out of here!" exclaimed David.

"Maybe we can hide under the tables," I said with haste.

"I'm pretty sure they'll still be able to get to us," he replied. "Keep running!"

We tried to run away, but the there was no place for us to go. There were no caves to hide in and the trees did not protect us from our inevitable encounter with the hawks. We had run so much that we reached the protective shield.

"I can feel the electricity," I said as I tried to touch the shield.

"There's no way out," said David. "We have to fight with them."

The hawks were getting closer to us. I could feel the wind created by their enormous wings.

"Quick… hide behind the bushes," I yelled.

David and I ran to the nearest bush, but I didn't make it. I could feel the feather wing tips of the hawk brush up against my back. One of the hawks had grabbed me from my shirt.

"David!" I screamed. "It has my shirt!"

"Grab my hand," David panted. David turned around and held out his hand while the hawk forcefully pulled me into the air.

I quickly grabbed David's hands. He dangled in the sky with me.

"Katrina, I'm going to spin myself in a circle. Hold on tightly!"

David threw his body clockwise to gain momentum. His legs started to twirl as he gained momentum. My hands felt his tug as I tried to hold onto him so that he would not fall. I started to feel dizzy as we spun in the air. I could see the other hawks being thrown into the sides of the golden-red shield from the wind that our spinning had produced.

I held on tightly to David so that he would not fall as we spun in circles quickly in the air. The hawk that held onto my shirt was spinning as well. The speed of the spinning caused the back of my shirt to tear. I could hear it tear little by little as we spun round and round.

"My shirt's tearing!" I yelled to David. David was making us spin faster.

"I've got it!" he yelled back. "I know what I'm doing!"

David spun even faster than before.

The back of my shirt completely tore off and we flew fast into the bushes. I was terrified that my body would get pricked from all of the bushes' branches. David let go of me and used his speed to quickly fall to the ground. It almost seemed like he was running toward the ground. He landed on his feet and seemed minimally affected by the fall to the floor. He extended out his arms and managed to catch my fall. My heart was pounding so fast that it felt like a drum being pounded over and over again.

There was no time to feel faint or anxious. I heard a horrific hawking noise. The hawk that had captured me was heading straight for us.

"It's coming for us! Put me down!" I yelled to David in fear. David quickly let go of me from his arms.

"There's no point in running," said David.

"We have to stop him," I said while thinking. "Fire! That's it… fire!"

"Whatever you mean by fire, it sounds perfect right now… come on… it'll be here in no time," he said.

I wanted to start a fire to scare away the hawk. I touched the bushes surrounding us and started a fire.

"Now, I know what you mean by fire," he said. "Let me get more branches to make it bigger."

"Sure," I said.

The fire grew as David quickly gathered branches using his speed and strength.

The hawk that was heading straight towards us looked fearful and turned back. It retreated to the golden-red shield where it had come from.

"It's gone!" I exclaimed with excitement.

"We did it!" shouted David as he hugged me really tightly.

I started to cry in both happiness and relief that it was finally over. I fell to the floor and sat exhausted with my knees bent. David sat next to me. We both looked horrible. We were drenched in sweat and our clothing had become ragged, not to mention my shirt being torn in the back.

Finally, the Council came to greet us.

"We are very proud of you," said the Protectin in charge of Continuity. "You have shown us that you are truly meant to lead us."

"Now that we know your powers, we will train you so that you excel in those powers," said the Protectin in charge of Training. "Tomorrow, you will start your training. Be here promptly at six in the evening."

Suddenly, a tornado surrounded David and me and we were separately taken away from the Sycamore Glen. Within moments, I was back inside my mother's living room.

"I'm so happy you made it through the challenges!" my mom exclaimed as she hugged me. "Let's get you cleaned up. Why don't you take a shower and put on some clothes that aren't so torn up." My mom started to giggle.

"I'm so exhausted," I confided in my mom.

"It would have been nice if you had told me what was going to happen," I mumbled.

"I don't get why everything's a secret in this house," I said as I slowly walked to my room.

I could feel torn pieces of my shirt swaying over my back. I couldn't wait to shower.

CHAPTER TEN

My mom had made me a huge dinner. I think she thought that I looked malnourished. As I set the table, I heard a car pull up the driveway. It was Jack with Amber and Robbie. My mom and I went out to greet them.

"What a wonderful surprise!" my mom said cheerfully.

"I dropped by so that Katrina doesn't need to take a detour on her way back to school," replied Jack while looking straight at my mom.

"Come on inside. I've made enough dinner for all of us," said my mom.

"Oh… thank you, Lorina. We don't want to impose," said Jack.

"Don't be silly! I insist," said my mom smiling with hospitality.

Everyone walked inside the house. Jack and Robbie walked into the kitchen to help get dinner set. Amber walked into the living room.

"Wow! These painting are stunning," said Amber in awe.

"My mom painted them," I replied. "My dad mostly carved artwork, while my mom painted and sculpted."

"Who did this one?" Amber asked as she pointed at an elaborate bronze sculpture of a heart with red crystals firing out around it. It was set on the side table near the sofa.

"I made that," said my mom.

"I designed that one when I first met Kevin, Katrina's dad," she continued.

"It's gorgeous! The crystals shine brighter than any that I have ever seen," Amber continued.

"Kevin gave me a bag of red crystals when we first met. He told me that it symbolizes our eternal love. He said that the red color in the crystals burns brighter than any fire raging in the path of lava and that our love burns deeper than anything that comes our way," explained my mom nostalgically.

"Awe... he must have been your soul mate," said Amber.

"Yes. It's been very lonely here without him. And, now that Katrina's living at school, I feel like I have a hollow hole in my heart," she continued as her eyes filled with tears.

"It's okay Mom," I said as I hugged my mom. "We'll find Dad. At least, we know that he's still alive."

"Amber, why don't you pick out anything in the room," said my mom. "I want to give it to you as a present."

"Oh... thanks Mrs. Swan," said Amber.

"Please call me Lorina.... We're not really formal in our household," she chuckled because she wasn't used to anyone calling her Mrs. Swan.

"I really love this sculpture," said Amber as she pointed at a bronze sculpture of a tree that was drooping down to touch the table. On the tree, there were a dozen blue birds scattered to form a heart.

"Can I have this one?" asked Amber.

"Sure... I had a feeling you may like that one. Some of my artwork can enhance the powers of the Protectins and Minders," added my mom.

"Really?" asked Amber.

"Yes. The crystals I use are from the volcano. With the right person, you will find that it will give you a boost in your powers," she added.

"What about the people that buy it from Jack's store?" asked Amber.

"They don't know what they are buying," explained my mom. "To them it's just another piece of artwork."

"Mom, I never knew you made these for the Protectins and Minders," I said surprised. "How do you give it to them?"

"Well, there's a storage area in the volcano that only allows Protectins and Minders. Over time, your powers will start to get stronger, but will get sloppy too. These crystals that I put on the sculptures realign your powers. It's kind of like a therapy method for powers that are really working well," my mom explained.

"These just happen to be my favorite sculptures," my mom continued.

"Is your power related to any of this?" I asked my mom.

"Hm… some of it is," she replied. "I have the power to heal and the power to build. Look!" she exclaimed.

My mom knocked a vase to the floor that caused it to shatter to pieces. She pointed her fingers at the vase. Within seconds, it rebuilt the same vase without any evidence of it having been broken.

"Wow! That's pretty cool Mom," I said. "I never knew you could do that."

"Why do you think we still have the same number of drinking glasses in our house?" she laughed. "I never bought new ones even though you made them fall all the time when you were younger."

I never realized it, but she was right. Everything in our house was always in pristine condition. Nothing ever seemed broken. My mom had just uncovered another secret in our household that was hidden from me from birth.

We went to the kitchen. I helped set more plates on the table and invited everyone over to eat. Jack and Robbie had helped my mom finish up the food preparation while we were in the living room.

Everyone sat at the dining table.

"Wow! Lorina, it ceases to amaze me at how delicious your cooking is," complemented Jack.

"Thank you, Jack. You always have loved my cooking," my mom said politely.

"Robbie, it seems like you are doing really well considering you are transforming," I said astonished that Robbie looked fine.

"My dad sprinkled a powder over me and it made my pain go away. I can't wait to figure out what my powers are!" exclaimed Robbie as he rubbed his hands together in anticipation and excitement.

"That's kind of what we need to discuss," said Jack. "Amber and Robbie are assigned to work for you and David. Considering that Kevin has been kidnapped, we need him to transform quickly so that they can try to locate your father."

"Doesn't it take three phases to transform?" I inquired.

"The process can be sped up if a Protectin wants it to be a quick transformation," added Jack.

"How can I do that?" I asked.

"Well, both you and David need to take him to the sacred Hot Springs where you will cover him with volcanic ash and have him swim in the warm water. He will have all of his powers within moments after all of the ash has been washed off of him."

"By the time I have David come here, Robbie will be fully transformed. So, I don't understand the point of having us take Robbie to the Hot Springs," I said logically.

"Well, if you have David come here using his super-speed, that shouldn't be a problem" Amber quickly added.

I had forgotten about David's ability to carry me quickly from place to place.

"I don't know if he can carry two people to Mammoth that quickly," I responded.

"He can try," added Robbie.

"Fine, I'll call him after dinner," I promised, giving in to the pressure.

After dinner was over, everyone pitched in to clear the table and wash the dishes. It was nice to have everyone help speed up the process.

I called David's cell phone.

"Hello. David! It's Katrina," I said on the phone.

"Oh.... Hi! I didn't expect you to call me," replied David. *"Are you okay after everything we went through today?"*

"I'm just really tired. I didn't expect it. I think it would have been different if I was prepared to face those challenges," I said.

"Well, I think we have to get used to it," added David. *"We're never going back to what we were before our transformation."*

"Did I tell you that Amber found her partner?" I asked in a very excited manner.

"Who is he?" asked David.

"He's a boy that I grew up with," I replied. *"His name is Robbie. I never knew he was a Minder!"*

"That's kind of cool," said David casually.

"Well... I found out that Amber and Robbie are the Minder leaders and that they report to us... and... well... you know... Amber and Robbie are our Minders... so...," I said hesitating to ask him to use his powers.

"So... what?" asked David, not being able to resist the suspense.

"Okay! I'll be upfront with you. I want you to help me get Robbie to transform quickly so that I can look for my dad. You have to use your powers to take both Robbie and me to the Mammoth Hot Springs. We have to rub lava ash on him and have him swim in the

130

Hot Springs so that he can transform quickly," I said without gasping for air as I spoke rapidly.

"I know you're upset that your dad is missing, but a couple of days are not going to make a difference in finding him. We haven't even learned how to fight yet," continued David.

"Every minute counts David," I explained.

"Fine. Why don't you come over to my room tomorrow morning?" David finally gave in.

"Thanks! Bye!" I said excitedly.

"See you in the morning," said David.

I put down my cell phone on the coffee table. I couldn't help being excited. I ran up to my mom and gave her a big hug.

"David said that he's going to get us to the Hot Springs. We're going to find Dad!" I exclaimed, with tears of joy rapidly falling down my cheeks.

"I hope so," said my mom, hopeful with reservations.

I was so happy that we were headed in the right direction. I'm sure we would find my dad soon enough.

Jack left to go home, while Robbie stayed behind.

"Robbie, you can stay in my room tonight before we go to David's room in the morning," I said.

We said good-bye to my mother and left for school. It seemed to take us a lot less time to get back to the dorm. There was no traffic on the freeway and time flew by as I listened to Robbie and Amber getting to know each other.

When we got to our dorm, Amber headed straight for her dorm room to sleep. She took her sculpture with her. Robbie followed me to my room. I didn't have much space for Robbie. He had to sleep on the couch in my room.

"I have an extra pillow and a blanket. Let me get it for you. It's in my closet somewhere," I said.

"Thanks, Katrina," said Robbie. "You have a great place here."

"Yeah, I like it," I said dreamily while I placed my hand in my pocket.

Robbie sat on the couch, getting ready to lie down.

"I didn't want to tell you this, but I feel like I have to," said Robbie with a low voice while looking down at his hands. "It's my fault your dad was kidnapped."

Robbie put his hands over his face and kept rubbing his head.

I quickly got out of my closet.

"What do you mean, Robbie?" I asked with my heart racing.

"Well, there was this guy who came by the store about a year and a half ago. He saw your mom's sculptures and thought they were beautiful. He asked me who made them and I told him your mom did."

"Go on...."

"Well, um... he kind of asked me where your mom lives. He told me that he's an old friend and would love to visit her. I didn't think twice and gave

133

him directions to your house. A couple of months after that, your dad disappeared. I think he may have been Tibeno."

"What!" I yelled. "He knows where my mom lives too!"

"I don't think he's going to do anything to her, Katrina. I mean... he would have done it by now," added Robbie.

"What do you mean? He's probably hanging out around my mom's house waiting to see what we're going to do. You never know, he may try to use her to protect himself."

Tibeno was evil and would do anything to take possession of the diamonds. I had to find David.

"Robbie...," I said softly so that I could calm myself down since Robbie was as panicky as I was. "I'm going to have Amber come over so that you aren't by yourself during you're transformation. Don't go anywhere until I come back. I have to go see David." I spoke quickly, without even taking a breath in between my words.

I ran downstairs.

I pounded on Amber's door.

"Hey!" yelled Amber. She was really cranky. "What do you want?"

Amber had woken up from my intolerably loud and continuous knocking.

"You have to go upstairs and watch over Robbie. I need to talk to David," I said impatiently. Amber looked dazed as I left her speechless in my haste.

I ran to David's dormitory.

CHAPTER ELEVEN

"David!" I yelled into David's window.

"David!"

He didn't seem to hear me.

I closed my eyes and yelled, *"Wake up, David!"* in my mind.

"David!" I yelled again out loud.

David came to the window. He didn't have a shirt on, which made me see his half golden diamond shining brightly on his belly button.

"We need to talk!" I said eagerly.

David looked groggy.

"Can't this wait till tomorrow?" asked David.

"We don't have time!" I was pleading.

"Fine. I'll let you in."

I ran to the front entrance of the dormitory waiting for David to open the main doorway. It seemed like it was taking him a lifetime to come to the door. I kept pacing back and forth in front of the door waiting for David. Finally, I saw him coming towards the door. He was fully dressed and ready to entertain my unexpected visit.

He opened the door really quietly so that other people would not wake up. I grabbed David's hand and pulled him to his room with great haste.

"We need to talk," I said breathlessly. All of my running and pacing had started to catch up with me.

We reached David's room.

"We have a problem!" I said loudly, without any consideration to anyone sleeping inside the dormitory.

David closed his room's door so that nobody would wake up from my loud panicking voice.

"Calm down, Katrina," said David as he placed both hands on my shoulders.

I couldn't relax. My heart was pounding so intensely that I felt faint.

"Katrina, just relax," David said again. This time he hugged me.

The warmth of his hug made my heart slow down its beats. I started to cry from all the stress that I had gone through in the past hour. David looked down at me and wiped my tears with his hands. He kissed my forehead.

"It's okay. I'm sure whatever it is, we'll be able to work through it," continued David.

At this point, I almost forgot why I had rushed to David's room. His warmth and the unexpected kiss on my forehead made my head feel dizzy. I didn't want to move. I only wanted to stay in his arms indefinitely.

Finally, I realized that David had diverted my attention away from the reason I had come to see him. I was starting to question the sincerity in his kiss and the loving embrace. What did he think I had come to his room for?

I sat down on David's bed. David sat on his desk's chair across from me. He rolled his chair next to the bed so that he could hold my trembling hands. I didn't want to speak, but only hold his hands. I had to fight my desire to be close to him so that I could focus on finding my father. It was a battle that I had to wage even though I wanted to hold his hands forever.

"David, Robbie told me something that we can't ignore," I explained softly and still distracted by his touch.

"And, that's the reason why you came running to see me?" laughed David as he let go of my hands.

"No, I'm serious. This isn't a joke David," I pouted. I was a little hurt that he let go of my hands first, though I know I didn't have the will to do it myself.

"Robbie saw a man at his store that knew my mom about a year and a half ago. He told him where my mom lives, and, sure enough, my dad was kidnapped. He thinks it was Tibeno," I continued, but now I was focused on the reason why I had come.

"This isn't what we need now," replied David, with his face becoming serious.

"I was at my mom's house yesterday and I'm sure Tibeno is staking out that place. He probably knows that I've already transformed," I continued.

"He's probably going to steal the diamond sooner than later," said David with a deep and upset voice. He stood up and looked outside his window.

"Katrina, I'm sure Tibeno knows we live here. He probably has people watching each one of us."

"What are we going to do?"

"Your mom has to leave her home. She can stay with my mom. I wouldn't want her to get kidnapped too," said David.

"I'm sure there are Mutineers around us too. We have to find them. If we do, we'll know where Tibeno is hiding with my dad," I said hopeful that we would find my dad soon.

"We can't wait until tomorrow to have Robbie fully transform. We have to go now," said David swiftly.

David put his hands around my waist and sped over to my room.

140

When I opened my room's door, Amber was on the floor crying.

"What happened? Why are you crying?" I asked.

"Robbie was upset … he went outside. By the time I followed him out, a man came and grabbed him. He put Robbie in his car and left. It all happened too fast for me to react!" Amber whaled as tears fell endlessly down her cheeks.

"So, now they have your dad and Robbie!" David yelled out while trying to think of what to do.

"I told Robbie not to leave! What was he thinking? Couldn't he wait for me?" I said while in a complete shock at the evening's events. "I should have kept Robbie next to me. I was supposed to protect him during his transformation."

David gave me a deep stare for a moment before turning to Amber. It seemed like he had a plan.

"Amber, do you think you can feel him?" asked David.

"I don't know. I haven't tried," responded Amber.

"If Robbie can still communicate with you, we may have a chance of finding him," said David.

"Why don't you try listening to his thoughts?" I asked Amber.

"I haven't done it before," answered Amber, "but, I'll give it a try."

Amber closed her eyes and looked very serious. A blue tornado like wind began to twirl around her. She raised her hands. The blue wind began to twirl faster with each passing moment. Suddenly, she brought down her hands and the wind disappeared.

Amber's blue crystal-like eyes glowed even more brightly than before. Her face, that once looked so concerned, now showed a glimpse of optimism. Amber was energized. Amber had found her ability to be a Minder. She was now complete and would be even stronger if she were united with her partner, Robbie.

"I was able to channel into the other Minders," explained Amber. "They told me that Tibeno does have Robbie and that they are headed to the Long Valley Caldera. We have to go there!"

"Tibeno isn't wasting any time," I said. "Now that he knows you and I are the leaders, he's heading straight for the diamond."

"We have to leave now!" exclaimed David, rushing to get out of the dorm and into my car.

"I'll drive," I told David, snatching my keys out of his hands. "Amber, you have to come too. We need you to find Robbie."

We all quickly rushed into my car, knowing that the outcomes of this trip may either destroy cities or get us what we want, my father and Robbie. Either way, we had no choice, but to go after Tibeno. Our fight training by the Council had to wait.

CHAPTER TWELVE

I was driving as fast as I could to get to the volcano. Luckily, it was night time and I did not encounter any traffic on the road. Amber was sitting next to me with her eyes closed trying to concentrate on what the other Minders were telling her. David was in the back seat trying to devise our plan. He was really silent.

"Katrina! They pulled over. They're in the city of Bishop," Amber said as she quickly opened her eyes.

I had been driving my car like a zombie race car driver, listening to the directions given by the navigation while my eyes were only looking forward at the road.

"Where are we?" I asked.

"We're only in California City! The navigation is telling us that there's over 200 miles left to get to Mammoth! Bishop isn't far from the volcano. It's only about 30 to 40 minutes away from there. Once they leave Bishop, they will be there in no time," cried Amber.

"At this rate, they'll get to the volcano before us," I sighed.

"Katrina, you're driving too slowly," David responded, as if he could drive any faster than me.

"Even if I did drive recklessly, it wouldn't make any difference other than getting us killed! We have over 200 miles to go to get to Mammoth. There's no way we'll make it there before Tibeno and Robbie leave Bishop," I said quickly, defending my driving capabilities.

"Do you know if Katrina's dad is with Tibeno too?" David asked Amber.

"Wait let me find out," replied Amber.

Amber closed her eyes again and a blue wind circled around her that got increasingly faster. I was used to the blue wind by now as she was frequenting it during her Minder information gathering sessions in the car.

"David, what are we going to do if my dad is there? We don't have any training," I said.

"I think we're just going to have to use what we know to get him back. We have no choice," said David.

"We have to work together telepathically," I told David. "We can't have Tibeno figure out our next move."

"I agree.... You and I are a team. We just have to trust each other," David said.

It was hard for me to really know how I could work with David as a team. The only time we had to work together was for the challenges that were set up for us by the Council. I didn't really know how we would work together for our first real mission. I only knew that I was attracted to him, probably because we were all supposed to be attracted to our partners. I had to remove my uncertainties and try to remember our goals of freeing my dad and Robbie and stopping Tibeno from taking the volcanic diamond.

Amber opened her eyes so rapidly that it was almost scary to look at her robotic gestures. She turned and spoke to us as if she was still in a trance of what she had seen and heard from the other Minders.

"Katrina, it seems like Tibeno does have your dad," said Amber.

"Great," I said with a sigh. "I guess we really do have a big fight ahead of us."

With my father there, Tibeno would definitely try to steal the volcanic diamond before we would make it to the volcano. We didn't want the diamond to be taken because that would mean so many lives would be lost due to the massive earthquakes and volcanic eruptions. The devastation would not stop until the diamond is regenerated.

"David, we need to fight," I continued sounding determined. I didn't keep my eyes off the road and made sure I was driving as quickly as I could, given the speed limit.

"Wait... there's more," added Amber. "Tibeno has a group of twenty Mutineers with him ready to fight. That's why he stopped off at Bishop. It's their meeting point!"

"We have to try to get to the volcano first," commanded David. "If they get there before us, we don't stand a chance."

"What do you suggest?" asked Amber.

"I'm going to push the car," said David.

"What?" I asked.

"You can't push the car," added Amber. "I get that you're strong and fast, but using your speed and strength to get us there quickly in a car doesn't sound realistic."

Amber let out a little chuckle in disbelief.

"Do you think closing your eyes are going to make us get there quicker?" David asked sarcastically.

I couldn't understand why their feud would not stop! I was tired of hearing the constant bickering.

"Stop," I said forcefully. "We're going to try out David's suggestion. I'm pulling over."

I pulled the car to the side of the two lane highway. It felt eerie being in the middle of the desert

148

with nothingness surrounding us. The only trees near us were Joshua trees.

David got out of the car and ran to the back of the car.

"You may want to make sure your seatbelt is on tightly," said David as he walked to the back of the car.

He walked swiftly and with confidence, knowing that he could carry the car. At first, David tried to see if the car was too heavy for him. I felt the car bounce up and down as David tested his strength.

Within moments, I felt the car tilt downwards towards the front as the back of the car lifted to the sky. David turned the car around while holding onto the bottom of my car's bumper. We were now facing the backside of the highway.

I looked out at my rear side mirror and saw that David was ready to pull us towards the volcano. He took a few steps and then he accelerated. I felt like I was going to fly out of the car. My body was thrusting forward since David had turned the car around. I held onto the steering wheel so that I wouldn't fly out of the car. I saw Amber pushing her body backwards by putting her feet flat on the dashboard of the car.

My heart was racing as quickly as the moving car.

The coldness of the air was magnified by David's speed. The noise of the wind made the evening feel more eerie than the darkness of the desert. My head kept on wanting to fly forward as I made a conscious effort to move it back towards the seat. I started counting in my head to help me from giving in to the pulling force of the acceleration.

"One, two, three…," I started to count aloud. I took a deep breath before I began counting again. "Four, five, six…" I started screaming.

I kept pulling my body back. I didn't realize how uncomfortable it would feel to be dragged backwards in a car that's going super speed.

Finally, I felt the car slow down. David was coming to a stop. I assumed we had reached the volcano, though I had no way of knowing. My head was spinning from the car ride.

David gently put the car down.

"No," whispered David.

I ran out of the car. As I turned towards the rear of the car, where David had been pulling the car, I saw what David had seen. There was a line of Mutineers blocking the road to the volcano. My father and Robbie were nowhere in sight. The Mutineers looked like normal people. They did not have golden strands of hair or blue crystal-like eyes; however, they had red crystals on their neck. Their eyes also had a red glow to them when they were ready to fight.

It was obvious that the Mutineers were there ready to confront David and me.

CHAPTER THIRTEEN

It was pretty evident that we were in Bishop. Tibeno had gathered about twenty of his followers to stop us from going to the volcano. Unfortunately, we did not know if Tibeno had left Bishop. We had to assume the worst case scenario.

The Mutineers were lined up in front of us waiting to fight on the road. It was so dark that I could not see their faces, only the red glow of their necks. The Mutineers were dark shapes in the night that were blocking the road.

I turned my head and looked at David. I started to speak to him telepathically.

"Is this the only road to the caldera?" I asked David.

"Yeah, Highway 395 is the only way that we will get there. We don't have many options," responded David.

"Tell Amber to hide and keep track of the situation with Tibeno. We can't let her get hurt. She's our only way of knowing what's going on."

It made sense for David to tell Amber. He stood next to her and could whisper our intentions.

"I agree. I'll let her know. Once she's out of the way, we'll need to confront them," said David while turning his head and looking at the Mutineers.

After our brief telepathic conversation, David softly told Amber to hide. I saw Amber running behind the bushes on the side of the road. I could still see her slightly because of the blue wind that she produced while communicating with the other Minders.

David and I got ready to fight. My heart was beating really fast. I did not know what to expect.

I started to think about my father and Robbie. I thought of how these evil people had taken them away from my life. I started to remember what the Council and David had told me about the volcanic diamonds. The thought of the Mutineers destroying the world for their own greed infuriated me so much that my anxiety went away and all I could feel was the need to restore the good in the world.

I looked at David and nodded my head.

I walked confidently towards the Mutineers. I reached out my hands and touched a tree to make it light on fire. I grabbed the tree and threw it towards the Mutineers. My hands were on fire. It seemed like I was an extension of the volcano. I had now become the flames produced by the volcano and was showing the Mutineers the devastation that it could bestow on others.

The flames had become a part of my hands. David looked at me with fear and awe. The red flames had given my golden hair an orange glow. They did not hurt my hands. They were a part of me. The Mutineers ran away from me as they saw me gradually approaching them.

David was already fighting some of the Mutineers. I could see David jumping up the air and kicking a Mutineer to the face. As another Mutineer approached him from behind, I saw David kicking that Mutineer backwards. Then, David grabbed him by his waist and threw him to the side of the road. David's strength caused the Mutineer to fly twenty feet away from him.

I had become so confident that no one would get near me to fight. I felt that the tree I had thrown onto the Mutineers had scared them off. Then, I heard a noise. I turned around and there he was, the Mutineer that would destroy the beautiful fire that I had produced on my hands. The Mutineer had a garden hose from a business on the side of the road and was spraying water towards my direction. I thought I would be able to dodge the water, but another Mutineer started to spray water towards me as well.

I was drenched. Worse yet, the flames on my hands had disappeared. My only physical power was paralyzed. I tried to make the Mutineers stop by using my power to change people's minds, but it did not work. Had the water turned off my powers? Was this my weakness?

I did not have time to panic. I was soaking wet! The flames would not come out of my hands. I no longer felt like I was a part of the volcano. I felt like a part of me was broken and that I had no way of repairing it.

I had to stay strong and fight through my insecurities. I could not let my weakness overcome my desire to save my father and Robbie.

Drenched from head to toe with the sprays of water continuously flooding my face and body, I knew I needed to get out of the situation fast. I could not let David fight this battle alone. He needed me as much as I needed him.

"David! Help me! I'm wet and I've lost my powers."

"I'm coming for you, Katrina! Just hold on...."

Then, I felt the floor beneath me crack open. The Mutineers holding the garden hoses were put off balance and the water was spraying up towards the

156

sky. I ran away from the Mutineers. I could hear the wet slosh of my jeans and shirts as I ran away from the garden hoses. My golden hair felt heavy. It was down to my waist as it had straightened from the wetness.

David was kneeling on the floor. His fist had hammered into the ground, which had caused the road to crack open.

"Run!" yelled out David.

I saw David running towards the Mutineers that had drenched me with water. He was going to ensure that they didn't water me anymore.

The other Mutineers noticed that David was preoccupied with the two that were hosing me down. They saw me running and started heading towards my direction. I kept on looking at my hands. They were still soaking wet! I needed to dry them off so that I could use my powers.

Five Mutineers caught up to me and encircled me. I had no choice but to fight without my powers. There was no sense in calling David for help. He was too busy trying to ensure the other two Mutineers would not disable my powers again.

Each of the five Mutineers was about three feet away from where I stood. Two of them were men that were almost two feet taller than me. The other three were very muscular women. They looked like they had been bred to fight.

I was the underdog. I had no powers and had never fought anyone before. However, I could not give up. I had to start thinking of why I needed to get through this situation.

As I had done before, I thought of my father and Robbie. Then, I thought of how Tibeno was about to destroy the lives of many people by removing the diamond. I kept on thinking of Tibeno's greed.

I started to get angry. I could hear my heartbeat. My body trembled. It started to shake off all of my wetness. I could hear the water drip to the floor like raindrops. I was now focused. I looked into the eyes of all five Mutineers. I turned my head slightly to see those that stood behind me in the perfect circle.

I knew what I had to do. I had to fight, even if I did not have my powers.

The first Mutineer, directly in front of where I stood, approached me and tried to kick my face with an axe kick that was headed straight for my face. I blocked his kick by quickly raising my right arm over my head. Then, I grabbed his foot with the same arm while it was in the air and kicked him in the stomach. This caused the Mutineer to bend his waist forwards. I then pushed him to make him fall to the ground.

The second Mutineer behind me thought that I would notice her coming straight for me. She grabbed me from behind with both hands. She held me tightly so that I would not move. I stepped on her foot and pushed my body backwards to make her let go of me. I then kicked her with my leg going back.

I quickly turned around and noticed two other Mutineers getting ready to hit me. I ducked down and they kicked each other in the air, right on top of me. I was glad that I managed to avoid the kick because I did not want to get hit in my head.

Just as the second Mutineer was straightening out to get ready to attack, the last Mutineer tried to make me fall to the ground by sweeping my leg with a low circular kick. I jumped up as if I were on a jump rope. The second Mutineer happened to be right next to me and fell to the floor because the kick swept her to the ground. The last Mutineer was upset. She looked at me fiercely because she had hurt one of her own.

I couldn't believe it. My powers had returned! All of the fighting had caused the water to dry off of my arms. My hair and clothes were wet, but my hands were dry.

I could feel the tingling sensation in my fingers. I ignited my fingers and jumped over the fallen Mutineers and to a tree. The last Mutineer that was fighting started to chase me. I found a tree and set it on fire. I pulled it out of the earth and threw it towards the last Mutineer.

I turned and saw that David was still fighting the Mutineers. It seemed endless. Our time was running out and Tibeno's distractions were doing their job. They were preventing us from going to the volcano.

"David, this doesn't seem to stop."

"I know. There are too many of them."

"I can create a path with fire. If we get them to stay on the other side, we will be free to leave."

"Don't worry. I'll keep them occupied," David said telepathically while giving me a smile as he looked at me from a distance.

I ran and grabbed Amber. I sat in the car and moved it up to an area away from the Mutineers. I saw a few Mutineers trying to chase me, but David was there to keep them away from the car.

"Stay in the car," I told Amber.

I ran to the nearest tree and created a horseshoe shaped path of fire on the road. Before I had finished the fire blockade, I called out to David.

"David!" I yelled. "Come over here! I'm going to finish it off!"

I had to scream because the noise from the flames were overpowering.

David used his speed to get through my last opening in the fire obstacle that I had created. Once David was safe, I lit the last tree on fire and closed the opening. We could now leave without worrying that we would have Mutineers following us.

I ran to the car. David had already started the car. I sat in the back and we drove off to the Hot Springs of Mammoth.

CHAPTER FOURTEEN

"Do you know where they are?" I anxiously asked Amber.

"They're already at the Hot Springs. They're walking towards the volcano's opening," Amber said with fear in her crystal blue eyes.

"We still have another fifteen minutes left to drive!" exclaimed David. "We have to ditch the car. I'll carry you two there."

I did not have any complaints. Anything to get us there quickly was the best option. Amber looked a little scared because the only experience she had with David using his speed to get us anywhere was on the car trip to Bishop.

David pulled over.

"Amber, stand next to me," I said. "Don't worry. It's really not a big deal. David always carries me places using his speed. It's not that bad at all."

I tried to comfort Amber, but she still looked scared.

David put one hand around my waist and another around Amber's waist. Then, we were off.

I could feel the wetness of my hair starting to dry out by the cool breeze caused from David's swift run to the Hot Springs. I turned and looked at Amber. There was a blue wind trailing from behind her.

Amber yelled, "Stop!"

David quickly stopped.

"I can't go any further!" she yelled. "Tibeno is in the cave heading towards the diamond. If an eruption starts and I'm there, I won't make it."

Amber was trembling with fear. She had turned completely blue.

"Just leave me here and go," Amber commanded. "I'll hide in the bushes."

Amber closed her eyes once again with the blue wind twirling around her, making her look like a blue unworldly beauty. We knew that she was trying to find out more about what was happening at the volcano.

"We can't wait for Amber to finish gathering data," said David. "We have to leave if Tibeno is already at the volcano."

"What if she knows something that we don't? What do we do then? We have to wait and find out what Amber knows," I replied, making sure that we don't leave without knowing everything.

"Then, I'm just going to have to go to the volcano by myself. You'll have to tell me what Amber finds out," said David being stubborn.

"Yeah… and tell me how I'm going to get to the volcano? It's not like I have a car anywhere around me. Do you think a forest fire is going to make me get there any faster?" I asked sarcastically. "Don't you remember the whole point of being my partner as a Protectin? We have to work together. What are you going to do if you need help?"

"I guess you're right. We have to watch out for each other," David said, regretting that he suggested going to the volcano alone.

Within a minute or two, Amber finished with her information gathering session. Her blue crystal-like eyes opened wide.

"You have to get Robbie!" she exclaimed. "Your father's in the volcano's passageway already, but Tibeno has tied up Robbie inside a dark place. Robbie's sweating from the volcanic heat. You have to go get him before Tibeno gets the star… otherwise, Robbie will definitely get blasted away."

"We have to hurry!" I cried out.

We had no choice, but to leave Amber. I hoped that she would stay safe, but how could I be sure with Tibeno's troop not too far behind us in Bishop? I didn't want Amber to get hurt. I was worried about Robbie. I didn't know if we were too late in reaching him.

David put his hands around my waist. Within moments, we were at the opening of the volcano at the Hot Springs. We must have dropped Amber off not too far from the volcano's opening.

"Where do you think Tibeno tied up Robbie?" I asked.

"I don't know. I wish we had asked Amber," replied David.

Anyone could tell that we were novices. I mean, how could I forget to ask Amber the simplest question? We didn't have time to go back and ask her now. Besides, Amber was going to hide. Finding her would take too much time.

"I'm sure Robbie isn't too far from here," David said.

"Robbie! Robbie!" I yelled.

I couldn't hear anything. It was dark and silent. The only thing that we could hear is the bubbling of the hot springs.

"We have to look for signs of an area where a volcano would explode from," I said. "Since this is a caldera, it can be anywhere. It's not like there is a mountain peak that's always going to produce the explosion like the volcanoes you see on television."

"How do you know these things?" David asked.

"I didn't have much to do at home, so I would look on the internet for how things are made in nature. I guess, it's starting to pay off now," I said with a smile on my face.

David and I left the opening of the Hot Springs cave. We were looking for anything that would show where the volcano would be able to explode from during an eruption. We examined the dirt, rocky floors to try and uncover cracks on the floor and openings. Unfortunately, since the volcano had not erupted for over a thousand years, the land looked undisturbed.

"There's nothing here," I said hopelessly.

"I'm sure it's somewhere and we just haven't come across it," replied David.

"Why don't we just split up? I'll look over here and you can look around the bushes over there."

"Are you sure you want us to split up? We haven't even gone on our first date."

"I didn't even know we were together." I started to blush.

David looked at me. I mean, he really looked at me. I needed to focus. We were getting off track. He put his hands on my shoulder and glided it quickly down to my hands. He held my hands with both of his hands.

"We'll find the crack. I'm sure we will. We just need to always stay together. Promise me that," he said.

"I promise." That's all I could say as I heard my heart beat pounding inside me. He gently let go of my hands. I felt so relaxed and almost like David and I were meant to be together.

We started looking for signs again.

I found a very thin crack on the floor. I don't know how I had seen it, considering it was so dark outside. The golden star on my neck only provided a little amount of lighting.

"I think I've found something!" I exclaimed out of excitement.

David turned around from looking behind some bushes a few feet away.   He rushed over to see the crack that I had found.

"We have to follow it," he said.

We followed the crack.

"Robbie!   Robbie!" I yelled, but no one answered back.

"Do you see anything?" I asked David.

"No, it's only shrubs and small trees," said David.

As soon as David finished speaking, he took a step and fell into a deep hole.

"David!" I screamed.

"David!" I screamed again.

"David!" I screamed, this time with tears falling down my faces as I knelt down to my knees crying.

I put my hands on my face crying. I had lost my father, Robbie and now, David. Was this my destiny? Were the people I care about going to slowly disappear from my life? I didn't want this to become my destiny. I needed to do something about it.

170

I stood up and faced the evening sky while my hands were extending out like an eagle extending its wings. My fingers started to go on fire as I cried with sorrow. I felt like my body was starting to spin. Slowly, I felt like my body could rise up off the floor. The fire on my hands raged, which gave me the strength to spin and rise up off the floor.

My sorrow turned into my own amazement. The golden cape embellished with stars appeared on my back. I was now a Protectin. Not just a regular Protectin. I was one of the most powerful Protectins. I was now in charge of changing the evil predicament that was bestowed upon us.

I felt the heat on my hands as the fire in my palms raged higher by the second.

I flew! I flew higher than the adjacent mountains. The fire on my hands lifted me off the floor. They gave my golden hair an orange glow and my soul a red flare of desire to find the ones I love.

I knew that I needed to enter the dark hole that David had fallen into just moments before the amazing discovery of my strength. I slowly descended with confidence.

"David!" I yelled.

I could not hear anything.

All I could see, as I entered the dark hole, were white magnificent crystals. They had a red glow as the fire on my hands illuminated them in the darkness. I could also see platinum and gold minerals as I descended into the hole.

"David!" I yelled again, after having descended about ten feet.

"Katrina," I heard back faintly.

I could hear David! I was so excited.

"I'm coming down to get you."

I slowly came down to an area that was flat. It had a slight downward incline, but not enough to make me slide down. It looked like I was in the sill of the volcano. It was a cave-like passageway of the volcano that had been created thousands of years ago from an ancient eruption. Unfortunately, if the volcano were to explode, the debris that had been created thousands of years ago would explode out of it to help the lava flow out of the volcano. I was certain that Robbie was in here.

"David," I said as I hugged him with happiness. I was overjoyed that he was still alive.

David looked like he was scratched up from the fall. His golden hair looked black from the black dirt he hit against the edges of the sill.

"Are you alright?" I asked David.

I lifted some of his hair to reveal a really bad scrape he had gotten on his head from the fall.

"You look like you had a hard fall," I continued. "I wish I had something I could do."

"I'm fine," responded David. He was still in a bit of a daze from the fall. His voice was weak, but strong enough to have called out to me.

"Can you walk?" I asked.

"Let me try."

He put his hand in mine so that I could pull him up off the floor. David stood up slowly.

"I think I'm fine." He still looked dizzy from the way that he walked.

"We don't have much time. We need to find Robbie," said David as he seemed to awaken from his moments of dizziness.

"Why don't you wait here?" I asked, concerned that David may have taken a hard fall down the sill.

"No. We should go together. We're a team, right?" David said with the dynamic voice that was once lost due to his dizziness.

I glanced at David to make sure that he was not going to tip over as we left.

We ran down the slightly sloped sill. We could feel the heat of the magma. There was a slight wind from the radiating bubbling heat of the volcano that caused debris to randomly hit us as we ran down the sill.

After running down the sill for about twenty feet, I saw Robbie lying on the floor tied up with a bandana over his mouth.

"Robbie! What have they done!" I shouted as I feverously took off the bandana.

David quickly untied Robbie.

"Tibeno threw me down the hole and I rolled all the way here," explained Robbie. "They're heading for the diamond."

"I'm pretty sure they don't have it," I said. "We would have felt the earthquakes."

I felt confident that we weren't too late.

"Actually, Tibeno should be on his way to the diamond now. Tibeno said that he was going to put your father in a trance because your father was refusing to retrieve the diamond for him. Tibeno has several men with him. They're talking about taking your dad back to the car and hooking him up to a machine that would let Tibeno take control of your father's actions," said Robbie.

"That means that we can't wait around here any longer!" I exclaimed as I grabbed both Robbie and David so that we could leave the volcanic sill.

We ran through the sill until we reached the vertical tunnel that Robbie and David had fallen into. I looked up at the dark hole that showed no signs of being friendly to climbers.

"How are we going to get out of here?" asked Robbie.

"Just watch," I said while giggling. I could tell that David had read my mind because he threw out a little smile too.

"Robbie, why don't you put your hands around my waist," I said.

"What?" Robbie asked, confused about what was about to happen.

He slowly put his hands around my waist facing me. He started to pull me closer to him.

I rolled my eyes and gave a deep sigh. I turned my back to Robbie and repositioned my hands. There was no need for him to get intimate ideas of me when all I wanted to do is get all of us out of the volcano's sill.

I opened up my hands. We began to spin. I could feel Robbie holding on more tightly as we spun quickly up the tunnel. The flames on my hands raged as I spun faster. Finally, I no longer needed to spin because the flames on my hands helped me ascend gracefully through the dark vertical hole until we reached the top of the tunnel.

"Thanks for getting me out of there," said Robbie. "I... I... um... thought you missed me."

"Of course, I miss you," I responded. "You've been the only real friend that I've had growing up."

"Yeah... don't you miss our hikes together and all the places we would explore in the mountains? I miss you more than I miss a friend, don't you?" he asked.

"I do miss you, but only because you've been my best friend growing up. I thought you and Amber hit it off. What happened?"

Robbie looked at the rocks below. He didn't want to answer my question.

I paused.

"I'm sorry…. I really need to go back and help out David," I said, not waiting to hear Robbie.

I did not want to hear about his feelings towards me. I turned away from Robbie, glancing back to see that he stood there with his sad blue eyes looking at the floor. Some part of me felt sad, but I had no feelings for Robbie other than that of a brother. He was the only one I ever saw growing up in Topanga. Even then, we saw each other very infrequently. I went down the hole to get David.

"I thought you forgot about me," said David laughing. "So, when did you figure out how to use your fire power to fly?"

"Well…," I said pausing for a moment. I didn't want David to know that I cried over him when he fell down the hole.

"I was really anxious when you fell down the hole. I somehow learned how to control my powers so that I could fly," I continued. I wanted to be brief.

David didn't need to know every detail. Needless to say, I really didn't know how he felt about me. He was always around Brenda at school, but he also flirted with me. I sometimes felt like David liked Brenda and only thought of me as a partner in his working Protectin relationship. I didn't want to be his back-up girlfriend. It's just too confusing.

"What do you want me to do?" he asked.

"You know what to do," I said laughing. "It's my turn to have your hands around my waist."

"Yes, it is," David said with a laugh.

It felt empowering to finally be in control. I was able to fly, while David did not have that ability. He was now able to feel the helplessness that I felt while he transported me from one place to another.

We went up the tunnel quickly. As we were flying up the tunnel, I heard an explosion. The explosion was followed by a forceful wind with debris that pushed us out of the tunnel. The wind gust was hot and so powerful that we were thrown to the floor several feet away from the opening of the tunnel. Our clothing was charred from the heat, and both David and I were scraped by the lava rocks that made their way out of the hole.

"It's starting Katrina… We need to go to the diamond now!" David exclaimed while being out of breath.

"What about Robbie?" I asked. "We can't leave him here. If the lava explodes out of this hole, he'll die. He's not fast enough to get away from the lava or the explosions!"

"I'm sure he can take care of himself," David said.

"Robbie!" I yelled.

Robbie was nowhere in sight. I did not want to leave him, but I needed to make sure the diamond did not get removed.

As we ran down the hill towards the cave opening, I saw Robbie running down the hill in the distance. I was certain he knew what was about to happen. After all, I am certain that he was starting to get his Minders' power. Maybe Amber had told him to leave. I did not have time to think about Robbie.

Nonetheless, I felt comforted that he was trying to quickly get away from the volcano.

CHAPTER FIFTEEN

"Hurry!" David cried out.

"I'm not as fast as you are. I don't have the luxury of having super-speed," I replied.

"It doesn't matter. We have to hurry up before Tibeno steals the diamond!"

"I'm really trying to be faster than normal David," I explained.

I was climbing over rugged rocks to get to the cave. In the distance, I could see the springs bubbling in the evening darkness. I was really tired of climbing over all the rocks that were in our way to get there. The fact that I was so close to the cave's opening made me overjoyed.

I quickly ran to the bubbling pool of water while forgetting about the treacherous journey to get there. The opening to the cave looked undisturbed by the movements of the earth that had been caused by the volcano.

We ran inside the cave to the red rock. David touched the rock, giving a glow to the golden star on his neck. The red rock opened up to the passage with the red crystals. There was no time to look at the passage in awe as I had the first time I had entered.

Once we were inside, we were running through the elaborate cave. We had to get to the Sancdia quickly. I heard a rumbling noise.

"No!" I screamed. "I think they're at the diamond."

"We have to hurry," said David with great haste.

All of a sudden, I felt a big jerking movement in the passage. David fell onto my arm, which knocked me over to the floor. I scrapped my jeans on the red crystal rocks on the floor. David managed to quickly stand up after having fallen on top of me. He gave me his hand and helped me up. I felt the pain of the fall. I could feel the throbbing of my knees and my thighs.

There was another jerky movement in the floor. This time, David and I were prepared and did not lose our balance. It felt like we were running through a cave with constant and unpredictable movements.

Without a moment to rest, the earth began to tremble. The floor looked like waves that we had to somehow climb over. The earthquakes had begun. I feared that Tibeno finally had the diamond.

The heat we felt from the boiling magma seemed to magnify with every wave created by the minor earthquakes. Hot lava rocks flew in our pathway as we ran erratically towards the room with the diamond. The earthquakes became more intense with every step that we took towards the room with the diamond.

Rocks fell from the sides of the cave as we ran in a careless manner. The earthquakes were causing us to fall and roll from side to side. We got used to dodging falling rocks from each tremor. We had to move forward. We had to pretend like the earthquakes were only objects in an obstacle course on the way to the finish line.

The seconds that we ran in the cave felt like hours. Each trembling earthquake felt like it lasted an eternity. Our hearts raced with each jerking movement, only hoping that the earthquakes would stop. It didn't stop. It only became more intense with every earthquake that passed through the cave.

The red glow of the cave no longer looked beautiful. It was angry. It was enraged at the fact that someone was trying to take away a part of the volcano. Someone had disrespected nature's balance. We had to reach the diamond before it would be too late for everyone.

David and I were so glad to have reached the Sancdia. The few minutes to get there felt like hours. I was ready to face anyone except my father. How could I fight my own father? Even if my father was under a spell, there was no way that I would hurt him.

At the entrance of the Sancdia, there were two members of the Council guarding the doorway.

"What are you doing here?" I asked firmly. There was a big jolt of movement on the floor as I questioned the Council members.

"Stay out of here," commanded one member of the Council.

"Stay out of here or you will regret it," said the other member.

"Never," said David firmly. "Get out of our way or you'll regret it!"

"There's no way we'll let you through. Tibeno is our friend. He promised to make us rich and powerful if we help him. I'm not going to let you stop me from becoming rich," said the first member. He was furious and determined not to let us through.

"You have an obligation to us," demanded David. "You're going to hurt people because of your greed."

"Let us through now!" I yelled.

Neither of the Council members moved. They had golden stars and golden hair just like me and David. They were not Mutineers, but rogue Protectins.

186

David and I had to strip them from their power. The only problem was that neither of us knew how to do it. We were still new to the Protectin world. Unfortunately, we did not have any time to explore the extent of our abilities.

We had to confront the Council members. There was no time to waste. The earth beneath us was rumbling louder than before. The heat of the molten lava was radiating everywhere in the passageway to the Sancdia. We had to get inside the Sancdia and stop my father.

"Get ready to fight," David said telepathically.

"Let's do it," I said anxiously and without moving my lips.

I pushed the female Council member to the floor, while David took care of the male Council member. The diamond star on my neck began to glow as I entered the Sancdia. I felt my powers magnify. The tingling sensation in my body radiated with heat, ready to face anything.

"I'm in!" I yelled to David. "Hurry!"

David ran in the Sancdia after I called out.

"Your father's trying to take off the diamond," he said in haste.

"I know," I said while running towards my father.

"Watch out!" yelled David. "She's behind you."

The rogue Protectins were ready to fight. They were determined to keep us away from the diamond.

The female Council member charged towards me. She tried to grab me by my hands, but I kicked her so hard that she fell down against the rocky wall. My cape let me spin quickly into the air so that I could let my hands glow with its familiar flames. I was now ready to use all of my powers against the rogue Council member. She got up off the floor and looked furious. She had a bolt of lightning in her hand, ready to let go at any moment.

The Council member threw the electrified lightning bolt directly at me. I placed both of my hands in front of me and let my hands release so much fire that the lightning bolt exploded, creating metallic red fireworks. It produced such a loud screech that I felt like I was electrified from the noise.

I continued to keep my hands out in front of me with the flames burning even stronger than before. I could see David fighting the other Council member. We had to work together. I wondered if I could do more with my power. I flew in the air and threw flames out to the Council member. I could see the magma boiling beneath the transparent floor. Every time I threw out a fire ball, the lava from below met my flame in the air. My fire was one with the lava. I was part of the volcano and all of its fury.

I flew over to David who was fighting an endless fight. I lowered myself to the transparent floor.

"David, hold onto my waist," I said.

David held onto my waist without asking any questions.

I flew into the air.

"Run! Run as fast as you can in the air!" I said excitedly.

"What?" David asked confused.

"Pretend like you are running on the floor," I explained more clearly. I was getting a little too excited and didn't seem to make sense.

"Oh...," said David as he started to run.

David and I were running in circles in the air. As David ran holding onto me, we created a large tornado of air. David ran faster and faster while holding onto my waist. I could feel his hands turning my body more rapidly with every turn.

The Council members didn't know what was happening. They were too confused to do anything. I threw out my fire balls. The lava met my fire in the air. The tornado was lifting the lava into the air and was growing larger with each spin. The speed that David provided from running made the lava rise up higher more quickly. We built a large wall of fire and lava. The tornado around us met the lava as if it were meant to be one. David and I had created a lava tornado around us. I brought my hands up higher and higher to let the lava tornado rise above us.

"David, look up!" I yelled as I held up my hands. "You don't have to run anymore. I've already built my tornado."

David still held onto my waist because we were flying with fire. He looked up with amazement.

"Wow! That's amazing," said David as he held onto my waist tightly. I could feel him holding on with more force as he looked up at my creation.

The Council members were looking up too in disbelief. I quickly thrust my hands forward and let go of the lava tornado onto the two rogue Council members. The lava tornado flew over them and, then, engulfed them completely. The lava was so heavy that it tore into the transparent floor and fell into the raging magma beneath the floor. The lava had taken the Council members with it to their doom.

I slowly flew down to the transparent floor. I was hot and drenched in sweat. My golden hair looked like sparkling treasures. David hugged me to comfort me when we reached the floor. He was as hot and sweaty as I was, but his heart was not pounding as fast as mine.

We were not done. We had to stop my father. My father had released three of the five sides of the diamond from the volcanic rock that it was hung on. He was on the verge of releasing the fourth side.

My father had a metal armor covering his head. His face was open. This must have been what was making Tibeno control my father. Tibeno must have been using his brain neurons to control my father's movements.

My father's face looked cold and unresponsive. The father I remembered was hidden beneath the trance that Tibeno had bestowed upon him. I could only see my father's beautiful brown skin and traces of his curly hair beneath the metal covering on his head. When I last saw my father, I had not transformed. So, the curly hair that I had once recalled as being brown was not the golden color common to all of the Protectins.

"Father! Stop!" I yelled.

"Kevin, please let go. We don't want to have to fight you," continued David.

My father ignored our pleas. He continued working on releasing the fourth side of the diamond. My father efficiently released the fourth side of the diamond from the volcano.

I could see the magma beneath us rise up higher and with more fury than before. The earthquake it produced was stronger and more destructive than the earthquakes we had felt inside the passageway to the Sancdia. Rocks were falling down from the walls of the room. The boiling magma was throwing flares of lava almost as high as the floor that we stood on. The volcano was getting ready to explode.

We quickly walked towards my father.

"Dad, don't do this please," I pleaded.

It didn't seem like my father had any remorse. He was working like a robot, quietly and efficiently. He continued to hammer away the rocks that were holding the star diamond in place.

193

"Katrina, I'm sorry, but I have to stop your father," said David quietly.

"No! I'm sure he will come around," I cried.

I approached my father and touched his back.

"Dad, please don't let Tibeno take the good out of you. You can't let him kill millions of people for his greed," I said crying.

As I spoke, there was a large tremor passing through the volcano. I could hear the rumbling of the boiling magma. It sounded like dynamite. My ears were becoming numb from the noise.

I grabbed my father by his back and cried with my tearful face touching his spine. He did not even seem to notice that I existed. David came to pull me away from my father, but something unnatural occurred. The golden star on my neck glowed as well as the ones on David and my father. We were now three leaders of the Protectins all touching each other to create the perfect and most powerful unison.

The glow of the star created an image of my father on the wall of the Sancdia. Although my father

194

was chiseling away to tear the last portion of the rock holding the diamond, his soul was projected onto the wall. It was as if my father was trapped in a robotic body and his only freedom came from the fact that all three of us came together as one.

"I'm sorry Katrina. This isn't me. It's Tibeno," said the image. "I don't want to bring harm to people. I am a Protectin like you and only want the good of people."

"Father, I know. But, how can we free you? I don't want to hurt you," I said.

"The only way you can save human lives is to strip me from my powers. It is the only way that you can defeat Tibeno," he said.

"But, you can't walk on the floor. Father, what will I do?" I asked.

"You have to do what is right. You need to banish my powers. I love you," said my father as the image slowly disappeared.

"I know it's hard Katrina," said David while holding onto my shoulders. His curly lashes glistened from the moisture in the hot room. The magma's heat was escalating to a point that even we were feeling its intolerable nature in our sacred room.

"Your father wants us to stop Tibeno. We have to protect the people," continued David in a soft and somber tone.

He was trying to comfort me, but it did not seem to help.

"I can't do anything to stop my dad from falling into the lava when we strip him from his powers," I cried.

"I know, but we don't have much time. Your father has most of the last portion of the rock chiseled away. We need to do it now," said David with great haste.

I was reluctant, but I knew that it needed to be done. Even if I created a lava tornado, I would not be able to save my father. He would become mortal and would die from touching the lava.

I wiped the tears off my face.

"I'm so sorry Dad. I hope that you will forgive me," I cried.

I held David's hands. We twirled in a circle in the high ceiling of the volcanic room. We rose higher and higher. The golden light illuminated around us as our golden capes floated in the air with us. I stared directly into David's eyes.

"We'll do it when you are ready," said David softly. He gave my hand a gentle squeeze.

"I'll never be ready, but we need to do it. I don't think we should wait any longer," I said with a tear falling down my eye.

We had never banished anyone's powers. However, it was innate to us because we somehow knew how to take away someone's powers. It was as if we were born with the knowledge.

David and I flew directly above my father. There was no fire on my hands, only the warmth of my dear friend's touch. We united all four of our hands together and aimed it directly at my father who was underneath us. We had created a golden stream of stars that penetrated into my father's soul.

Red flashes of lightning came out of my father as he methodically chiseled away at the rock. The lightning became more intense as we continued to direct the golden stars at him. I cried as I saw my father slowly start to leave his hammer and slowly melt onto the floor.

Once we stopped aiming the stars at my father, he fell quickly. He was no longer able to stand on the transparent floors.

I was so anxious that I instantly started to fly with my flame driven hands. David grabbed onto my waist so that he wouldn't fall to the floor. There would have been no way that I would have been able to reach my father in time for him not to melt in the lava. I didn't know, however, that by David holding me, I could fly ten times faster than normal.

Within a few moments of the fall, David and I were able to grab my father from falling into the lava. He was only two inches away from reaching the angry magma beneath him. We flew him to the passageway leading to the Sancdia.

"Do you think my father is alright?" I asked David as I took off the metal armor from my father's head.

"I don't know. We need to let him rest here on the floor, while we put the diamond back in its place," David said caringly.

I carefully lowered my father's head onto the floor and then followed David into the Sancdia.

"The diamond is about to fall off," David said with great haste.

"Yeah… my dad did a good job taking it off," I replied snickering.

If my father had chiseled one more piece of the rock, the diamond would have been taken off of the rock. David and I looked at the diamond. It was almost going to fall off. We put our hands outside of the diamond, but made sure not to touch it. Our hands created a binding force that quickly mended the rocks holding the diamond. Pieces of the missing rocks magically came together like a puzzle.

While the diamond was being reinforced into its original place, I saw the magma below the transparent floor slowly calm down. The rumbling noise almost became nonexistent. The earthquakes had stopped. The volcano was, once again, at peace.

"Katrina, let's take your father out of here. Maybe, Tibeno hasn't left," said David.

"I'm going to take the head armor too. It may come in handy," I said.

"Why?" asked David.

"Amber and Robbie may need it. I'm sure there's more out there than just Tibeno. This is only the beginning for our fight," I continued.

David grabbed my father and put him over his shoulder. I had forgotten that David was really strong. He didn't even seem to mind that he had a heavy body over his shoulder. The only sweat on David's body was from the heat of the molten lava.

When were outside of the cave and next to the springs, there was no one in sight.

"I'll go and look around for Tibeno," said David. "You stay by your father."

"I'm sure he's gone by now," I said doubtful that Tibeno would still be around.

"Well, we still need to try," said David, sounding like he had given up hope too.

David left us to look for Tibeno. It was very quiet. My father had still not woken up from his unconscious state of sleep. I looked at my father. He looked so peaceful. The golden curly haired man that was working intently on releasing the diamond, now had the dark brown hair that I once remembered. I wondered if he would remember anything that had happened. Do you forget everything once you are banished?

The darkness of the evening was slowly going away. We had been out all night trying to stop Tibeno. Watching my father's peaceful sleep made me want to lie down on the rugged rocks. I felt my eyes get heavier as I sat there watching my father. It didn't matter that the sun was peaking over the majestic mountains. I was tired. My body was aching from all the fighting and my soul was comforted at having found my father. I closed my eyes for a moment.

CHAPTER SIXTEEN

I woke up in my room at my parents' home smelling like smoke. I looked in the mirror inside my room and saw that my golden wavy hair had become black with all the volcanic ash. My jeans and shirt were ripped and I had small scrapes all over my body. I must have gotten them from all of the fighting that we had done in the evening.

The clock on my nightstand said that it was already one thirty in the afternoon. I couldn't believe it was that late in the day. I had probably slept around four in the morning.

Amber was lying down on the floor next to my bed. She had a pillow and a soft, furry blanket. Her skin was flawless, making it noticeable that she had not physically fought any of the evening's battles. Nonetheless, I was glad that nothing had happened to her while we were inside the volcano.

I walked around my room and saw David sleeping on the other side of my bed. He too had a furry blanket and a pillow. I'm certain my mother had covered up both Amber and David.

Despite all of the scrapes on David's body, he still looked handsome. I knelt down next to David. His golden hair had covered the injured area on his head. I pushed his hair to one side and stared at the wound he had gotten from falling into the volcanic opening. I slowly and softly stroked his hair. David opened his eyes.

"Hey," said David.

"Hi," I said softly so that Amber would not wake up. "Your wound looks pretty bad. Does it hurt?"

"Just a little," he said. "We both look like we had quite a night. What an evening," David giggled as he recalled the evening.

"We got you father back," said David with a smile.

"Yeah. Did you find Tibeno?" I asked him.

"No. I couldn't see a car anywhere. I think he just took off after the earthquakes stopped. He probably knew we put the diamond back," David replied.

"You were knocked out by the time I came back. I left you there with your dad and ran back to get the car. I picked up Robbie and Amber on my way to picking up both you and your dad. By the time we got to your parents' house and put your father on the sofa, we were exhausted and just decided to stay in your room. Your mom gave us some blankets. I think we got here around eleven in the morning. I'm still tired. Do you mind if I just sleep?" asked David.

"No, please… sleep. I didn't mean to wake you up. You can sleep in my bed if you want. I don't think Amber's going to be jealous. She's knocked out. I'm just going to clean off your head wound first," I replied.

David got up and went on my bed. I went to the bathroom and found antiseptic wipes to clean off his head lesion so that it wouldn't get infected. David was asleep when I got back to the room.

"Wake up." I gently pressed against David's arm.

"Yeah… I'm awake."

"I'm just going to clean off the wound on your head, okay?"

"Okay."

"Ouch," cried out David when I cleaned it off with a cleansing wipe.

"Sorry. I know it hurts, but I don't want you to get an infection."

"Don't worry about me. I'm fine," he said while trying to close his eyes to mask his pain.

I carefully cleaned the lesion to make sure there weren't any remnants of dirt left on the area. I put on some antibiotic ointment and bandaged it up carefully. He had taken a really hard fall down the volcano's sill and I was happy that nothing happened to him. I couldn't imagine losing him. We were always going to be together. I'm not sure if we would ever have a real relationship, but I knew he would always be my closest friend and my "partner".

David fell asleep almost instantaneously after I cleaned off his wound.

Although everyone in my room was asleep, I needed to take a shower. I quietly took my clothes out of my drawers and headed to the bathroom. I don't think anyone would have woken up even if I had the music playing in the bathroom. My clothes were so ripped that I would not be able to salvage them. I took them off and threw them in the trash.

It felt so good to finally cleanse the dirt off my body. I could see black water on the floor of the shower from all the volcanic dirt and ash on my body. Finally, the water was clear.

I looked at myself in the mirror after I showered. My golden hair shined more beautifully than ever. I wondered if my father would be able to see the golden color or if I had robbed him of his privilege. He was banished from his powers, which meant that he would not be able to keep any of his Protectin powers. I wondered if that meant that he would not even be able to identify a Protectin in public. I know that if we had retired him, he would have been able to use some of his powers, like telepathy, but nothing too significant.

Amber and David were still asleep when I got out of the shower. I closed the curtains so that they could sleep in for a while. As I shut the curtains, I noticed that Robbie was not in my room. What had happened to Robbie?

I went to the kitchen to get some cereal.

"Good morning Mom," I said.

"Or, do you mean good afternoon?" she asked while chuckling.

She gave me a big hug.

"I'm so glad you're alright. I can't believe you found your father. Last night, we felt all of the earthquakes. I knew you were at the diamond. The newscasters said that the Mammoth Mountain volcano was about to erupt. They were also saying that there was a weird incidence of volcanic unrest around the world. I was hoping you would be alright. When the earthquakes stopped, I knew you did not let Tibeno take the diamond. I'm so proud of you."

She hugged me again.

"Ouch. Not so hard," I said to my mother as she hugged me. "I'm a little sore."

I grabbed a box of cereal and went to the refrigerator for some milk.

"Did Dad wake up?"

"Hello, sweet pea," said my father as he walked into the kitchen, surprising me with a hug. He looked unharmed and like he had always looked. His light brown skin had no scars and his brown curly hair shinned with the daylight sun peaking into the kitchen. He did not have any star on his neck. He looked normal and without any special powers.

"I'm so happy to see you!" I said with excitement. "Do you remember anything that happened last night?"

"Of course, I do! Just because you banished me of my powers, it doesn't mean that I lost my memory too. I just won't have any powers... ever."

"Can you see my golden hair?"

"No, I don't have any powers at all, Katrina. I'm sure it looks beautiful, but I can't see your golden hair or anything else. It only looks like you dyed it blonde.... Sweetheart, you look like my beautiful daughter and nothing less... the way you always have." My father came over and gave me a big hug.

"Without you and David last night, there would have been so much destruction. So many people would have died. I'm sorry for putting all of you through that nightmare. I didn't want to do it, but Tibeno's men put the metal armor on my head to control me."

"David told me that he couldn't find Tibeno after we stopped you from releasing the diamond," I said.

"Tibeno left a long time ago. Even if you had gone outside while I was chiseling off the diamond, you wouldn't have found him. I heard him tell two of his men to transport the diamond to him."

"Do you know where he was headed?" I asked while I munched on my cereal.

"His base is in Malibu Canyon. I'm sure you won't find him there even if you looked. He was packing up before he took me to Occidental College to get Robbie. I guess he wanted to be close to Topanga Canyon when he set up his operations. I am certain that he was planning this attempt of robbing the diamond for quite some time," explained my father.

My dad reminded me to ask about Robbie's whereabouts. I felt guilty that I had forgotten about him again.

"Where's Robbie?" I asked, interrupting my father.

"I called Jack to pick him up when David got here," replied my mother. "I'm sure he's sleeping comfortably in his own bed."

I was relieved that Robbie was with Jack. Robbie had a rough night too after being tied up in the volcanic sill.

I finished up eating my cereal and put my dishes in the dishwasher.

"Mom, I'm going to go to Jack's," I said. "Let David and Amber know that I won't be too long when they wake up. I want to borrow some of Robbie's clothes for David. His clothes are really torn. I don't want the students at school to have suspicions."

"Sure. I'm certain Robbie will be asleep too," my mom said.

"Oh…. Wait! Can you give Jack this sculpture I finished making? It will save me the trouble of going there tomorrow." My mom looked like she was in a hurry.

"Okay," I said as I waited for my mother to get the sculpture from her studio.

She quickly came back with more than one sculpture for me to take to Jack's store.

"I'll see you later," I said as I headed to my car for a little drive in the mountain to Jack's place.

CHAPTER SEVENTEEN

When I arrived at Jack's store, Jack was outside polishing the brass outdoor sculptures. Robbie was nowhere to be seen.

"Hi Jack!"

"Katrina, I'm so happy to see you!"

"My mom sent over these sculptures for you." I gave him the sculptures.

"How's Robbie doing? My mom told me that you picked him up when we got home."

"He's fast asleep. I don't think he'll be awake for another few hours. He had a few scratches here and there, but nothing too serious. Robbie was telling me that he tripped over some rocks when he was running away from the volcano. Amber found him just a few feet away from where she was."

"I had a feeling they would find each other," I said.

"So, what brings you here?"

"I… um… I came to see how Robbie's doing."

"That's nice of you. Do you want to come in and have some soda?"

"Actually, that would be perfect!"

We walked inside the store. There was a door that separated the store from the back part where Jack and Robbie lived. Jack unlocked the door and went inside to get me something to drink.

"Don't be shy. You can come in. I don't think Robbie will be awake for at least a couple more hours. Nothing can wake that kid up… believe me, I've tried!" laughed Jack.

"Well, what about the store? There's no one at the cash register."

"I don't get many customers in a given day. Besides, we can drink our sodas and chat outside… Come on… I want to show you something."

I followed Jack inside the long hallway. We passed the living area, kitchen and Robbie's room. Robbie was fast asleep. He wouldn't wake up even if a truck's horn blasted in his ears.

The last room down the hallway was locked. Jack took out his keys and unlocked the door.

"I thought you should see this room. I've wanted to show it to you since you were in high school, but your dad thought it was too early," he said.

I walked inside the room. It was full of highly sophisticated computers everywhere.

"I showed Amber this room when we she met Robbie for the first time," he continued.

"Is this the control room for the Minders?"

"Actually, it's a little more than that…. You see, each one of these computer connects to the brains of the Minders. When the Minders transform, I bring them here and make sure that they're connected to the Minders' network."

"How do you do that?"

"Let me show you."

I followed Jack to a separate room that opened with the touch of his hand.

"The Minders need to stand in this room with their partner. Once I leave the room, I program the computer database outside to unify the thoughts of the two Minders. This allows them to telepathically communicate with all of the Minders."

"Did you do that to Robbie and Amber?"

"Yes, although Robbie was not fully transformed, he was still able to hear Amber. However, he couldn't hear the network. In a few hours, Robbie will be fully transformed and will be able to hear the communication between all of the Minders. If Robbie wants to speak to Amber privately, he can still do that because he's still connected to her as well," he said.

"It must be tough hearing all the conversations of the Minders in your head," I replied.

"They'll get used to it. I did... it just takes practice to tune everyone out. Robbie and Amber have a tougher job because they need to know what everyone is talking about."

"That must be impossible to do. How could you possibly remember what everyone is talking about?" I raised my eyebrows in disbelief.

216

"They can. They were born with a super processor imbedded in their brains. This lets them remember everything that's communicated among the Minders without distracting their daily routine. Let's go back to the control room. I'll show you their brain sequences."

Jack and I walked to the control room. He sat down at the main computer. He was typing so fast in a coding language that I couldn't make out what he had commanded the computer to do.

"See." Jack pointed at the computer screen. "This area here is the genetic difference between the Minder leaders and the rest of the Minders. When I had Amber and Robbie in the room, it confirmed my suspicion that they were both leaders."

"What do they do with all of this information?" I asked.

"They give all of that information to you and David. You'll know when to ask them for it. In fact, since Robbie and Amber now report directly to David and you, both of you have the ability to directly communicate with them as well. You don't only have telepathic powers with David, but also with Amber and Robbie. You'll know how to communicate with them… it's genetics." Jack seemed very casual in his responses.

"Once I show Robbie and Amber everything, I can finally retire from my duties," added Jack with a sigh. He seemed like he was ready to leave his position.

I saw the metal headpiece that my father had worn at the volcano in a box in the corner of the room.

"How did that get here?" I asked Jack.

"David gave it to me. He wanted me to analyze its contents."

"Did you find out anything?"

"The components of the headpiece indicate that there's been a Minder working on its creation. No Mutineer would've been able to have access to data that would allow them to create a headpiece to control someone's mind, let alone that of a Protectin leader!"

"There must be other rouge members.... I wonder how many Tibeno has gathered in his group."

"I don't know Katrina, but you and David have to get to the bottom of this or else they will take control. That won't be good because I'm sure they will treat humans like slaves if they have their hands on the diamond and the power that comes along with it."

"I'm going to head back," I said with haste as I walked toward the entrance of the store. "Thanks for the soda!"

"I'll bring Robbie over when he wakes up.... Hopefully, it won't be too late at night. I have some things that I want to go over with all of you. There's a place I want to show you that will help you find Tibeno."

"I can't wait!... Oh, can I borrow some of Robbie's clothes for David? His clothes are pretty torn up."

"Sure... let me just grab some for you." Jack quickly ran inside to get a pair of jeans and shirt.

"Hey... thanks for the clothes!" I exclaimed.

"Sure, anytime," he said as he handed me the clothing.

I quickly walked to my car.

"Bye." I waved to him. Jack waved back.

I got in my car and drove up the windy roads to my house. Amber never told me about the control room. Maybe she never got the chance because we were too busy looking for Robbie.

Everything Amber did now seemed to make sense to me. I just had to make sure I knew how access the information I need from her when I need it the most.

CHAPTER EIGHTEEN

I had spent a couple of hours at Jack's store. After having spent my time in the control room, I was pretty certain that Tibeno's goal of stealing the diamond had not changed. By the time I came back home from Jack's store, David and Amber were in the kitchen.

"Hi," I said surprised that they were awake.

I walked over to the breakfast table and sat in between David and Amber.

"Did you sleep well?" I asked.

"Yeah... I needed it," said David as he stretched out his arms.

"I would have slept better if I had your bed," snickered Amber. She was still very mean to David. I could not understand how she could work with us wholeheartedly if she did not get along with David. I had to fix this. It was getting out of hand.

"I brought some of Robbie's clothes for you," I told David. "You can take a shower in my bathroom."

"Thanks," said David as he finished eating his cereal. "I think I'll go do that now. I can't wait to take a hot shower."

He grabbed the clothes and went to my room.

"Amber, feel free to grab anything to wear from my drawers," I offered.

"I think I'll wait until I get back to change," said Amber.

"I don't understand why you're so mean to David," I said boldly. "That whole transformation thing is over and we all have to work together."

"I know. I just don't like him." Amber had a very cold demeanor.

"Why? It's not like he's done anything to you."

"I don't know why you're blind to the fact that he's a jerk," she replied.

"But, he hasn't done anything to you," I said defending David. "You really need to put those feelings aside. You're going to have to work with him even if you don't want to."

Amber puffed and rolled her eyes. Maybe she was jealous that I was spending so much time with David that I had completely neglected our friendship.

"Amber, you're still my best friend. I really haven't had a best friend with a girl before. Sure, Robbie was the only person I saw, but it wasn't like I could tell him everything," I assured her.

"David's a part of me now. Even if I hated him, I would need to somehow get over it... our powers coexist," I continued.

Amber took a deep sigh.

"I'm sorry. I wish that we didn't have to have this whole pair thing in the Minders and Protectins. It's too hard to keep up with the friendships you have when you have to work with someone you don't like all the time. I'll try to be nicer to David. I know he's a part of you."

I was glad that Amber was finally being honest with me. I suppose she was not mentally ready for the responsibilities of a Minder. It did take a lot of time and energy. We weren't the normal teens. Imagine going to college and, instead of spending time studying and partying, we had the responsibility to stop people from taking a diamond which would cause a disaster.

I still had not gotten use to all of my responsibilities and I could imagine that Amber felt the same way. Only a few months ago, I didn't have to worry about Tibeno stealing a diamond that would cause mass destruction! I was living in my own happy world, something that turned out to be an illusion.

"I went over to Jack's shop," I said to change the subject.

"How's Robbie?" asked Amber. "He didn't look really good last night when I found him. I think that he may have twisted his ankle because he had tripped over some rocks near the place I was hiding. He was really weak."

"Robbie was asleep. Jack said that he looked fine and that he really needed to rest. It's hard for him because he hasn't fully transformed," I explained.

"I can't wait until he has all of his powers. I'm sure we can do a lot when we both work together," added Amber.

"That's exactly it! You need Robbie to be more precise in what you do and I need David to be more powerful in what I have to do. It's not much more than that," I said trying to persuade Amber to be civil with David.

I was lying. It was much more than a power-driven relationship. Of course, I liked David! Who wouldn't? He was charismatic and caring. His voice brought shivers down my spine. The only problem was that I didn't really think he felt the same way about me. Brenda was my reason for my doubts. He always hung out with her at school. I didn't want to make a fool out of myself. I would have rather hidden in my world of indifference than to admit my true feelings.

"Jack told me that he wants to show me a place not too far from here. He said that it will help us. We have to wait until David gets out of the shower. I'm sure Robbie is about to wake up also," I continued.

"Sure. I guess.... If that's the case, I'll borrow something from your room when David gets out. Do you mind if I shower too?" asked Amber.

"Not at all... um... there's a bathroom in the hallway you can use. I'll get you jeans and a t-shirt from my room. You don't need to wait for David to finish showering in my room's bathroom," I replied.

Amber continued eating while I went to my room to get a change of clothes for her. The room's door was open, so I figured it would be alright to go in.

David turned off the water when I walked into my room. I was really nervous that he would open the bathroom door when I was in there rummaging around for some articles of clothing.

I couldn't help being clumsy around my room. I constantly dropped so many jeans and shirts that were hanging on my hangers. I felt like a thief in my own room trying to be quick. My hands were quivering with nervousness.

226

As soon as I finished gathering all of Amber's change of clothes, David opened the bathroom door. I tried to run out quickly so that he did not think I was in there waiting for him to finish. As I turned away from my closet, I tripped over a pair of shoes on the floor. I felt like a fool.

"Hey, are you alright?" David said while rushing over to help me.

He was putting on his shirt as he rushed over. His hair was dripping wet and smelled like the lavender shampoo in my shower.

"I'm fine. I accidentally tripped," I said.

"I can tell…. So, you know how to fly, but you don't know how to walk," laughed David.

I half grinned, more out of embarrassment than because I thought it was funny. After all, how could I not fall? It's not like any other guy had ever showered in my bathroom before, not to mention one that I actually liked.

"Hm… maybe, I should fly out of here," I said wittily from embarrassment.

I quickly ran out of my room and to the kitchen.

"Here you go," I told Amber as I handed her the change of clothes.

"Are you alright? You're out of breath," she said.

"Yeah.... I just tripped. It's not a big deal," I said. "Do you need me to show you to the hall bath?"

"No, I'll figure it out," said Amber as she grabbed the clothes and glided out of the kitchen.

I left the kitchen and went to the living room. I sat down on the sofa wondering where my parents were. I looked outside from the living room window across from the sofa and did not see their car. They must have gone out to eat. Maybe they went to their favorite organic restaurant in Topanga to celebrate their reunion. It was almost dinnertime. Here we were eating breakfast at dinnertime. My entire timing for the day was gone.

I put my head back on the sofa and closed my eyes. It was nice to be all alone. I had not been alone for a long time. Ever since I started Occidental, it seemed like my days raced by like a road runner.

Having grown up in the mountains and being homeschooled, I was used to being all alone. Having a moment by myself seemed more precious than any diamond on any mountain. Tibeno had it all wrong as far as I was concerned.

Unexpectedly, something made the sofa jolt. Was there another earthquake? Startled, I opened my eyes.

"You scared me!" I yelled, while David jumped off of my sofa and onto the couch next to me.

"How can anything scare you?" asked David with a giggle.

"What are you talking about?" I asked confused.

"Well…. Now that we have all these powers, we can do anything. No one can even think about getting near us," he continued.

"Are you serious?" I asked sarcastically. "It's not like we're invincible!"

"Think about it, Katrina. We took on so many men yesterday or last night... whatever, it was.... We can do so much more," he said.

David looked confident as he sat next to me. His eyes looked power hungry.

"People look up to us now," David continued. "We have to take down Tibeno.... When we find him, just promise me that you'll fly instead of walk."

"Whatever," I said blushing because he was referring to the incident in my room. "I was thinking about Tibeno too! I went to see Jack today to talk to him about it," I said.

"You didn't go for my clothes... ha, ha, ha...," laughed David.

I took the pillow and threw it at David.

"Funny! Okay.... I went for both," I said playfully.

"Seriously, Jack's coming over pretty soon to show us some place that will help us find Tibeno," I added.

"Can't wait!" said David as he got up to go to the kitchen. "I think I'll grab some of your mom's cookies before we go. She was baking them before you got here."

"Where are my parents anyway?" I asked.

"Oh, your mom told me to tell you to lock up after you leave today or tomorrow. She said that they were going to go on a little trip," he said.

"Seriously…. She told you and not me! She could have at least texted me!" I exclaimed.

"You'll get over it," laughed David as he went to the kitchen to grab some of my mom's cookies.

CHAPTER NINETEEN

By the time Jack arrived, it was already six o'clock. It was getting dark outside and there was no sense in going hiking at night. Jack knocked on the door.

"Hi.... Come on in," I said to Jack and Robbie as I swung the front door open.

Amber and David were sitting on the sofa in the living room.

"Hi," said Jack.

Robbie went straight for the living room chair. He did not bother to greet anyone. He still looked like he was half asleep. Jack probably woke him up and dragged him to my house.

"We all need to get going," said Jack. "I have to show you the Dome. We need to leave now."

"It's pretty late. Can't we go tomorrow morning?" I asked.

"No, we have to go now. This is the perfect time to go to the Dome; otherwise, you won't find it."

"Does it move?" I laughed while asking the question.

"Yes," Jack replied coldly.

"That's cool!" David said jumping off the chair. He looked excited about going to this mystical place.

"If we don't leave now, we'll miss the entrance," Jack insisted.

We all headed straight for the door. After all, we did not want to miss going to a place that had an entrance that moved. Jack told us that we needed to walk to the Dome. It was supposed to be very close to my parents' home. Apparently, my parents had bought the home based on how close it was to the Dome.

"The Dome is the center of all communications among the Protectins and Minders," explained Jack. "The volcano is the meeting place and the location of the sacred diamonds, but it is not where you will access all of your information."

"I wish Kevin could have shown it to you, but since you took away his powers, I have no choice but to do it myself," continued Jack.

"What about the control room that you showed me? Isn't that where the Minders access the information?" I asked confused about what he had shown me earlier in the day.

"Yes and no… the control room is where the Minders have their information network. It gives them the ability to share information with each other. The Dome is where the information is gathered to share with the Protectins. It's a little different. The control room is Minder to Minder and the Dome is Minder to Protectin." He wasn't sure if I understood.

"I get it." I wanted to reassure that I understood the difference.

"How do you know how to get there?" asked David.

"Only the Protectin and Minder leaders know where it is located. I was a leader for the Minders and worked closely with your mother and Katrina's father," said Jack as he looked at David. "My partner was my wife. She's no longer with us. We used to come up here every weekend and make sure

234

everything was alright…. Ah… those were the good old days."

We walked through the forest for about thirty minutes. Jack seemed to know the place really well. He did not need to leave a trail for us so that we would not get lost. He knew exactly how to get there.

The sun was almost done setting. Our flashlights seemed more important to me now than finding the Dome. I could hear the howling of the coyotes as the dark seemed to engulf the entire forest.

"Jack, are you sure you know how to get back?" I asked. "It's not like we can see anything in the dark."

"Trust me. I have been here so many times," Jack said as he put his hand on my shoulder.

"You said that we lived close to the Dome, but it's taking so long," I whined.

"Come on, Katrina. You should know these hills better than any of us," said David.

"Yes, but…" I said.

"Yeah, don't you remember us hiking these hills in the summer, Katrina?" questioned Robbie. "We used to run around while our parents would take a stroll behind us. Sometimes, we used to lose them and create games until they found us."

"I do remember. You were the only real friend I really had. I used to wish your parents would bring you over more often so that we could play with each other. It was so infrequent that every moment I saw you felt like an eternity. I never saw anyone else," I reminisced about my lonely past with only Robbie as my "friend".

Amber could tell I was about to break down crying. She put her hand around me as we walked endlessly into the dark forest.

How was it that I was deprived from all the joys of a friendship as a child? Was being a chosen Protectin child worth it? Did David have the same past? David never complained about growing up isolated from everyone else. It seemed so natural for him to make friends at Oxy. I couldn't understand why I was so different. Now that I had friends, real friends, I knew that I never wanted to go back to that isolated world ever again.

"Katrina, not everyone is the same. We all have our chosen paths," said Jack, sensing that I was uncomfortable with my childhood. "Your parents did the best to raise you. If they had raised you in the city, Tibeno would have found you and made sure that he destroyed all of our powers for his greed."

"I'm sorry you didn't get to go to school like me," added Robbie. "I guess your parents may have been a little paranoid.... Hey, if I didn't have school, I would have been around you more often." Robbie winked and smiled.

David looked agitated.

"Yeah.... I would have been around you if I lived here too," interrupted David. "I'm sure we would have had fun chasing each other in the forest too!"

"Too bad for you," responded Robbie with a slight snicker.

I began feeling less pity for myself and more discomfort during the course of the conversation. I should have stopped complaining. At least, Robbie would not have revealed his slight infatuation with me. It was even worse that David had to hear Robbie's feelings towards me. I couldn't believe that David was actually jealous. Amber looked agitated too.

I think I should have just kept my thoughts to myself. Now, everyone seemed to be irritated. There was a dead silence and everyone had a straight face.

I couldn't take the tension.

"Look... Robbie and I are friends! Nothing more," I boldly stated.

I didn't want Amber to be upset because I knew she really liked Robbie.

We walked for a few more minutes in the quiet stillness of the night. All I could hear was the cracking of the branches on the floor and the crinkling of the dry leaves. Then, we saw a magnificent light in the distance.

"We're here," said Jack with a smile on his face. "No one other than the Protectin and Minder leaders can see this entrance."

"It's beautiful," said Amber.

Amber was the only one who spoke. The rest of us were in awe at the sight of the magnificent entrance.

The enchanting entrance to the Dome was an unimaginable sight. The entrance was oval, slightly taller than my height. It was covered in golden diamonds with blue crystals outlining the outer edge of the entrance. The glow of the diamonds was so luminous that it felt like it was projecting images of gems onto our clothing. The diamonds looked like stars twinkling in a random pattern.

Jack walked into the entrance without any hesitation. We were too mesmerized by the entrance door that we did not want to walk inside it like Jack had done moments before.

"Come on," said David. "We can't stare at this entrance forever. What if it disappears?"

David had a point. What if the entrance disappeared and we did not get to see what was inside this magical Dome? We would have walked all that distance to no avail.

David walked inside the entrance.

The entrance stood out in the forest. There was nothing around the oval entrance other than trees. I couldn't understand how David and Jack entered the Dome, since there was no tangible building behind the entrance.

I hesitated for a moment, but followed David into the Dome. Amber and Robbie came in soon after me.

The Dome was unlike anything I had ever seen. The ceiling of the Dome was a semicircle made from volcanic rock. Red and gold crystals were embedded in the volcanic rock, making the ceiling glisten like a clear night sky full of twinkling stars. The room was lighted with golden lanterns hanging from the red rock walls. The floors looked like blue chunks of diamonds pieced together, giving it a bright glow in the, otherwise, red colored room.

Jack and David were standing in the left corner of the round room. They were next to a set of controls. I walked over to Jack.

"David and Katrina, this is where you will be monitoring everything that is happening with the world's volcanoes," Jack began to explain. "Although Tibeno only encountered you at the Mammoth Mountain volcano, there are so many others that he could have targeted. As you know, the Mammoth Mountain volcano contains the largest diamond, which can produce the most devastation if it is removed. The other volcanoes can also trigger large eruptions."

"Do you remember the story about Pompeii? History may only be revealing a part of the story of that volcano's mass destruction. People always imply that it was just Mother Nature, but there have been many other defects besides Tibeno in our past. Your job is to stop them from destroying our world and the people in it," he added.

I had never thought of volcanoes as having so much power.

"These are the controls," continued Jack.

There was a golden counter with four simple diamond switches. Jack waived his hands over the diamond switches and a more complex keyboard appeared. It seemed like everything was hidden. The room only looked simple, but when the real controls appeared, it became a chaotic place full of flashing knobs and transparent screens throughout the round room.

Amber and Robbie walked in as all of the real controls appeared. They were mesmerized by the colorful lights and undefined chattering noises of the transparent screens. Some screens showed randomized pictures of the volcanic diamonds. Other screens showed people walking around in different parts of the world.

As Jack started to explain to David and me the meaning of each one of the knobs, there was an explosion! Our jaws dropped from disbelief. All of our screens showed the explosion and we knew we had to do something about it. There was only one person who we knew would be responsible. Within moments, we heard another explosion. Our transparent monitors showed the fires and rocky avalanches. Tibeno was blowing up mountains and starting wildfires!

"Oh…. Nooo!" I exclaimed. The words seemed to take a long time to finish. They froze in the bitter sound waves that I had created.

"I'm sure it's not your parents!" exclaimed Jack.

"Katrina, let's get out of here!" responded David. "We have to help them…."

I was shocked from disbelief that my parents were trapped in an avalanche of rocks.

CHAPTER TWENTY

Jack guided David and me to another door in the Dome. When we entered into the new room, I saw two golden boat-like vehicles in the room with two seats in each vehicle.

"I know you can fly Katrina, but you will need these to bring back your parents," said Jack as he pointed to the two flying cars.

"These vehicles are only designed to be used by Protectin leaders. It took me years to perfect the design," continued Jack. Jack was proud of his accomplishment.

"Cool!" exclaimed David as he eagerly sat in one of the flying cars.

"I'll show Amber and Robbie what to do here. Robbie has all of his powers now. They will help guide you," said Jack.

"How do we start this thing?" I asked Jack.

"You need to control it with your mind," said Jack. "You'll get the hang of it."

"This is awesome!" shouted David as he quickly rose off the ground.

The ceiling of the room opened up as David made his way out of the room.

"Wait!" I yelled. "Aren't you forgetting me?"

I would have used my normal flying powers to out-speed David, but I needed the vehicle to bring back my parents. I knew I could not fly solo on this trip.

The flying cars were so fast. We knew that my parents were headed towards Northern California. However, we didn't know where they were located at the time of the explosion.

As David and I flew over the coast of California, we could see numerous areas of rocks slides over the highway. There was an inferno of fire raging around the rock slides. It would be very unlikely that anyone would have survived Tibeno's explosions.

I heard Amber's voice in my ears. She was communicating telepathically with me from the Dome.

"Katrina, you are about five hundred feet away from your parents. You need to go through the canyon to your right. They will be on the left side," said Amber.

I turned right. David soon followed me into the canyon. The canyon was dark with the thick smoke from the raging fire. It smelled like burnt charcoal from a barbeque. I was not afraid of the fire. After being able to produce my own fire on my hands, the flames around me did not scare me at all.

"David!" I yelled because the wind generated from the fire was so strong and loud. "Amber said that my parents are on the left side. You check the top part of the mountain and I will fly below."

"No! Don't go down there!" he shouted. "Robbie told me that there is nothing but flames down there. If your parents are down there, they wouldn't have survived. It's too dark. If anything happens to you, I won't be able to find you."

"Fine. I'll cruise at this level and you look for them on the top of the mountain."

I didn't exactly do as I said. I descended low enough so that I would not be trapped in the flames. The smoke was so thick that I could not see much around me. The darkness of the evening added to my impaired vision. Maybe, it was not such a good idea to fly at a lower altitude. I could not see anything anyway.

"Mom! Dad!" I shouted. All I heard were the raging flames around me.

Suddenly, I saw a part of a red car. The rocks had covered most of the car's front hood. The other areas were covered with dirt. Luckily, the flames were not near it yet.

"Amber," I called out to Amber telepathically. *"I found my parents. Can you pinpoint my location for David so that he can meet me here?"*

I could hardly breathe. The smoke was thick and I was afraid that my parents would not have survived breathing in the dense smoke.

When I approached my parents' red car, I could see that the front windows were only open slightly.

Half of the car was crushed by a pile of rocks and dirt, exposing several sharp metal pieces of the car's jagged-edged hood. Only the front window had a small area for air to pass through. Hopefully, it was enough to keep my parents alive.

As I flew next to the car, I noticed that a dozen red roses were thrown over the rocks and dirt. They were placed adjacent to the area where my mom sat in the car. There was no doubt that Tibeno had thrown the roses on top of the car. It angered me that he knew that my parents were in the car. It was obvious that this was much more to Tibeno than stealing the volcanic diamond. He did this to seek out his revenge for my mom marrying my dad. I was now more passionate than ever to find Tibeno.

"David!" I cried out, as I saw him approaching me in the haze of smoke. "I found them…. We need to get them out!"

David moved his vehicle close to mine so that we could speak to each other without having to shout.

The fire's roar made it difficult to hear, but the closeness of our vehicles let us speak without yelling.

"I can carry your parents' car out of here, but I don't have much room to stand. I can't drive and hold the car at the same time," said David, while trying to determine how we could move the car.

"I'll carry you," I said excitedly. "Remember... I know how to fly," I added almost like I was showing off.

"Fine, but you need to be careful not to set the gas tank on fire with your burning hands," he replied.

"I'll try," I said laughing.

We parked our vehicles on a very small ledge next to the car. There was not much room left on the hilly road. Most of the road had been torn apart from the sporadic rock avalanches.

I felt the burning sensation in my arms. My hands began to flare, similar to the fires that were surrounding us. David put one of his hands around my waist as I began to lift myself off of the two passenger vehicle. I flew next to my parents' car.

"Go down a little lower," said David.

The car was parked next to the edge of a cliff. I could not imagine how David would be able to lift the car with a ton of rocks blanketed over its vibrant red colored hood. I'm certain that the dirt and smaller rocks throughout the rest of the car also added to its heavier weight. The rock avalanche continued in small waves. There were enough rocks that they were able to cover some of the roses that were thrown on the car.

I heard a loud noise. It sounded like a tree had fallen from the raging fire in the mountainous area above the car.

"Hurry!" I exclaimed.

"I need to be closer... to be able to lift... the car," replied David with breaks in his voice from trying to reach for the car while holding onto my waist with his other hand.

"Got it!" exclaimed David with enthusiasm.

He lifted the car with his one hand. As I ascended above the thick smoke, I could not even feel the weight of the car. I tried to keep my flaming hands

250

away from the car by pushing my hands down towards my waist. The rocks fell off the car like a meteor shower in the thick smoke.

We quickly moved above the thick smoke. The flames from the burning trees felt so close. The raging fire made me feel like I was ascending to heaven and away from a deep inferno. As I flew upwards, I could see the beauty of the morning light beginning to peak out from the thick smoke. I simply wondered how long we had been looking for my parents.

Suddenly, I heard a rumbling noise from the burning hillside next to us. The burning trees were uprooted from the hill and fell tumbling down. The huge boulders above them violently fell down the hill too, colliding into more burning trees.

I looked below me and saw our two vehicles explode as the trees and rocks came crashing down on them. My heart palpitated as I realized that we may have been too late in saving my parents and ourselves if we had left minutes later. I took in a deep breath as I flew the car into an area that was not burning at the top of the hill.

After having landed, David gently put the car down onto the flat area of the hillside. We could see the raging fire in the near distance, but were far enough not to be harmed by it.

"Do you think they are alive?" I said as I looked inside the crushed window.

"I'll take off the roof and we'll find out if they are," David replied.

The top half had been crushed and I desperately hoped that my parents were still alive. David tore off the roof with ease. He pulled back the roof as if it were an orange peel.

My mother and father were covered in black soot.

"Mom! Dad!" I cried.

There was no sound from either of my parents in the car.

"I think they are alive," David said after looking to see if they were breathing. "I think they're only unconscious."

"We have to take them to Jack," I said in a rush.

"The car's tires are flat," noticed David. "I think I'm going to have to carry them."

Our vehicles were destroyed by the burning trees and rocks. David was our only way of getting my parents back to the Dome.

David tore off the top of the roof completely. He placed it on the floor. Then, David ripped off the back seat of the car and two seat belts. He put my parents on the back seat and tied them with the seat belts. This way, they wouldn't be able to fall.

"I can run back quickly, Katrina," David said confidently. "Fly back as fast as you can."

I agreed. David was strong and fast. He would be able to get my parents back to Topanga quicker than my flying.

Tears started coming down my eyes. I was overwhelmed by everything that had occurred throughout the day.

David approached me quietly. His golden hair looked as black as the burnt tree barks in the near distance.

"Don't worry. Everything will turn out alright," he said as he gave me a gentle hug. The charismatic voice that once embraced me was now endearing.

I started to cry. My body was trembling.

"You have to go," I said, still crying as I gently pushed him off of me.

"Hey… you have to stay strong. I'm sure they will wake up. They just need to get out of this smoke."

"I know, but they don't look like they're fine."

"Don't worry, alright," David said again as he quickly picked up the back seat and ran off with my parents.

I knew that I needed to follow him, but I needed a moment to myself. I needed a moment to gather myself before I faced the reality of the day. I kneeled down on the floor and watched the wildfire destroy the beautiful hillside. I needed that moment to think. I needed it to plan. I needed to find Tibeno.

CHAPTER TWENTY-ONE

When I got back to the Dome, the private entrance of the Dome was no longer there. Jack was not lying when he said that there was a very limited time period for the Dome's entrance to be visible. David was kneeling down next to my parents, who were situated on a white sheet on the floor. Jack was applying different types of ointments on their bodies.

Amber and Robbie came out of the invisible door that would normally be the pathway into the Dome.

"Katrina, I think they will be fine," said Jack. "They don't have any injuries. The smoke just knocked them out."

"Have they woken up yet?" I asked.

"No, but I am pretty certain they will be fine," he said. "I'll show you."

Jack pulled out an oval object. He scanned my father's body with it first.

"See! The readings all came out normal. They have only passed out from all of the smoke they inhaled. The lungs are even clear now in this reading," said Jack.

He then scanned my mother's body.

"It's the same thing. The best thing for them is to let their body rest," continued Jack.

"They must have ducked down in the car when the rocks started coming down the hill," added David. "They are very lucky to be alive."

"Jack, please take care of them. David and I need to find Tibeno before he does something else," I directed.

"Robbie, go get my car so that we can take them back to my house," commanded Jack.

Robbie ran through the woods to get the car.

"I'm going to stay with Robbie," said Amber. "If you need anything, you can always let me know." She grinned.

"What happened to the vehicles?" asked Jack.

"Um…," I hesitated to answer.

"You don't have to tell me," Jack sighed. "I'll give Robbie and Amber my design so that they can work on making another one."

David and I walked back to my house. I was glad to be alone with him so that we could have a chance to talk about how we would be able to capture Tibeno.

"Did you notice that Tibeno started all of this chaos pretty much after we got our powers?" I asked David. "Do you think he knows something we don't?"

"I'm sure it's only a coincidence," he responded. "He was going to try to steal the diamond anyway."

"Well, I mean, we haven't really figured out how to use all the stuff we have available to us. He knows that we're just novices," I added.

"Yeah.... Maybe, he doesn't think we'll know how to stop him. Maybe, he thinks he can get away with it," David replied.

"I don't think we should go back to my house or our dorm rooms," I said.

"What? We can't live in your car," laughed David.

"No…. I think we should go back to the volcano," I clarified. "I'm sure there's more there than we know."

"The Council will help us…. At least, if there isn't another rogue member," snickered David.

"I can't trust the Council. I think we need to be there by ourselves. If the Council comes in, we need to tell them to leave. I can only trust Amber and Robbie. After having seen the two Council members betray us when my dad was chiseling away at the diamond, I don't think I can trust the other members now," I said.

"I think we will need to select our own Council after this is all over. We need a fresh start," I added.

"Alright, it's worth a try," said David.

We got to my house and went in for a brief moment before leaving for Mammoth.

"I need to shower before we go. I smell like burnt toast!"

"This time, you'll have to go to the one in the hallway. I'm taking a shower too, but in my own bathroom," I added.

We took quick showers so that we would not waste valuable time. My beautiful golden hair revealed itself again after the warm water washed away the ashes. I felt tired, but refreshed.

There was no time to sleep, even though we had not slept all night. We had to find Tibeno before he caused another catastrophe. I couldn't believe that within a week, David and I had found my father, seen the devastating effects of removing the diamond, and saved my parents from the horrific explosions caused by Tibeno.

I was sitting on the couch in the living room when David got out of the shower. He slowly came over to me and sat on the chair next to me.

"Katrina, I think we need to keep an eye on your house. Everything that has happened has involved your parents. Maybe, he's lurking around your house or has someone staking it out," said David.

260

"That's a good point. I'll let Amber know so that Robbie and Amber can keep an eye on it when we leave," I said.

I telepathically told Amber so that we don't have any more strange things happening at my house.

"So, do you want to fly there?" I asked David.

"Do you want me to carry you to get there quickly?" he winked in response.

"Wait, before we go, I'm going to grab a couple of your mom's cookies. She really knows how to bake," said David as he quickly got out of the chair. "I'll get you one too."

I was exhausted and maybe some sugar would help me wake up.

When he came back from the kitchen, we were ready to leave. I decided to fly solo. David could manage getting there just fine. I couldn't imagine him carrying me to the volcano anymore. Flying with flames on my hands was more fun than being carried at super-speed. I could twirl in the air and do flips. The things I could do were endless. I felt free.

We arrived at the volcano. I quickly landed. I had really gotten used flying. It was effortless for me to go anywhere now.

"Remember, we need to tell the Council to leave," I reminded David.

We walked into the passageway that led to the sacred room, the Sancdia.

"We have to explore every part of the Sancdia," I said.

"I don't know if there's much in here. Maybe it leads to other rooms we don't know about?" added David.

As we walked into the Sancdia, our golden robes magically appeared on us. Every time I walked into that room, it felt like I was getting stronger. The boiling magma below the Sancdia seemed to give me more strength than I ever had before.

"Good morning, Superiors," greeted the Council as they came in one by one through the door inside the Sancdia.

"Good morning," we answered in unison.

"Is there anything that we may assist you with," asked one of the Council members.

"Um… actually, we're here to make sure that the diamond has not been touched," I quickly responded.

"No one can get near the diamond," said a Council member.

"We're fine here," said David abruptly. "You can leave."

David went to the door and opened it so that the Council members would leave the Sancdia. One by one, they went through the doorway and into a dark glowing tunnel. David did not close the door until all of the Council members had disappeared into the long hallway. Then, he slammed the door shut.

"There has to be something here," I said.

"Yeah…. I'm sure we're missing something," David said as he started touching the walls to see if anything would move.

"Hey! What if what we're looking for is in that hallway that the Council went through?" I asked.

"I guess we have to go and look," said David boldly.

David opened the door. We walked through the dark hallway that looked like a cave made from black lava rocks. There were platinum and gold pieces of rocks revealing themselves in the thick lava rock walls of the hallway. The hallway was not as elaborate as the passageway that led to the Sancdia.

Towards the end of the hallway, there was a split in the passageway. The left passageway had no barrier blocking anyone from going through. However, the right passageway had a frosted barrier with crystals and gold all around its outer edges.

"I'm pretty sure the Council went to the left," said David.

"I wonder how they know we're in the Sancdia so quickly," I responded.

"We don't have time to find out. Let's go to the right and see where that leads us," replied David.

"How do you open this thing?" I asked as I tried to push the frosted door open.

As I finished speaking, my hands went through the frosted glass.

"Oh!" I exclaimed. "It's not a real door!"

"Hey! Look at all the mirrors!" exclaimed David as he walked through the fake frosted glass door.

"There's so many of them," I commented.

Each mirror on the rocky walls was the size of a shoebox.

"They all seem to be showing volcanoes," I continued.

"Not all of them."

David faced the right side of the wall. He pointed at the wall in front of him.

"These are major cities around the world."

"David, look at this…. I can zoom in and out of the mirror."

"Where is Griffith Park?" I asked the mirror.

The mirror moved its view to Griffith Park in Los Angeles.

"Hey…. Let me try this," said David. "Where's Tibeno?"

Nothing happened.

"Wishful thinking!"

"Yeah…. It would be nice if it told us, huh!" laughed David.

"Show me my house," I said.

The mirror zoomed in on my house. There was complete stillness around my house. Nothing seemed to have changed.

"What's that?" asked David. "Zoom in closer."

I zoomed in on the side of the house and saw a small black box on the gutter above the front porch.

"Can you get any closer?" David asked eagerly.

"No, that's about it," I replied.

"Change the angle."

I twisted my hand to make a circular motion. The picture in the mirror's screen moved in the direction of my fingers.

The black box had metallic horizontal lines in the middle of the box. There was nothing else unusual about the box.

"Do you think that Tibeno put it there?" I asked while pointing at the box.

"I don't know, but we have to monitor it," David said. "I'm going to see if Robbie and Amber can figure out what that box is."

David walked to the other side of the room so that he could explain to Robbie and Amber what we had seen. I decided to leave the mirror showing my house and explore the rest of the room.

As I moved around the room, I felt like I was in the outdoors. All of the mirrors had sceneries of the volcanoes around the world. Each mirror would change pictures every few minutes. The greenery was beautiful. The mountains looked peaceful and undisturbed.

Towards the back of the room, the walls narrowed and shortened. There was a small passage that I could only crawl through. I got down on my knees and crawled through the passage. The more I progressed towards the end of the passage, the hotter it became. I finally reached the end of the passage. It seemed like there was a solid wall at the end of the crawl space. I felt disappointed that nothing came out of my crawl.

I touched all the rocks around me with the hopes that they would do something magical so that my trip was not worthless. The rocks felt smooth despite their rugged look. I guided my fingers from one rock to another. My fingers disappeared inside one of the rocks. I put my entire hand through the rock. The rock was just an illusion!

I bent down further so that my head could fit through the illusionary rock. When I peeked through the hole, I saw another room with lava flowing above it.

The room was ordinary with the exception of the lava that was above the room protected by a clear shield. There were red rocks with black dust piled up in different areas of the room. I entered the room with curiosity.

The heat of the lava flowing above the room was overwhelming. As I approached the red rocks, I noticed that the black dust was actually platinum that looked black due to the dark red lighting of the room. I picked up one of the red rocks.

"Ah!" I yelled and dropped the red rock.

When I had picked up the red rock, the lava from above dripped onto the rock, stopping after it reached the rock. Once the rock had contact with the lava, the lava stopped dripping onto the rock and seemed to flow again above the room in complete harmony.

The rock began to change form. The red dirt on the rock boiled away from the heat of the lava. I watched the rock from a distance as the lava slowly flowed off of the rock, revealing the inner layers of the rock. As the lava reached the floor, it created a small area of smoke and dissipated into the air. It looked like there had never even been any lava on the rock or the floor beneath it.

Once the lava had cleared off all the layers of the rock, the only thing that was left was an oval gold ball the shape of a football. I picked up the rock that was, surprisingly, not very heavy. I examined the golden rock. I turned the golden rock over and saw a series of seven buttons.

"I have to take this to David," I thought.

I quickly crawled back to the room with the mirrors.

CHAPTER TWENTY-TWO

"What is that?" asked David as he looked at the golden oval rock.

"I don't know. If we press one of these, I'm sure we'll know," I responded while turning over the rock to the side with the buttons.

"Where did you find it?"

"There was a little passage at the end of this room. I'll show you later." I pressed the first button.

When I pressed the first button, the rock turned into a keychain with a small mirror. On the back of the mirror, there were seven buttons labeled one through seven. The mirrored keychain was small enough to fit in my pocket.

"Look! I can see the outside of this volcano in this mirror," I enthusiastically said.

"That's pretty cool!"

"I'm sure it can do much more."

"Hm.... Show me Katrina's home," David commanded the small mirror.

The mirror showed my house. Then, I pressed the second button.

"That's cool!" yelled David.

The mirror created a transparent shield around me and David.

"Wow!" I exclaimed enthusiastically.

"I can't put my hands through it." David smiled as he attempted to put his hands through the shield.

The small mirror keychain was still in my hand. I pressed the third button.

The shield was only around David.

"Ha, ha, ha! I have you trapped."

"It's not funny! It's getting really hot in here." David was pounding on the shield to get out.

"Calm down.... I don't know what these other buttons do...," I was thinking about whether I should press the fourth button.

I didn't want to take the risk. I pressed the first button.

David fell to the floor drenched and red from the heat that was inside his personal shield. I dropped onto the floor next to him.

"I'm sorry…. I didn't know that was going to happen," I explained as I knelt by David.

"Just don't point that thing at me again."

I needed to find out what would happen with the other buttons, so I turned to a mirror on the wall and pointed the small mirror key chain towards it. I pressed the fourth button. The shield quickly appeared. The mirror inside the shield had frozen icicles on its edges. As I waited, staring at the mirror, there was an intensity of heat that abruptly melted the ice and caused the mirror to shatter into pieces. Once the mirror shattered, the shield around the mirror dissipated.

I pointed the keychain at the shattered mirror. I pressed the fifth button and the shattered mirror pieces began to boil.

"Press the sixth button," cried out David. He was finally sitting up from having fallen to the floor from heat exhaustion.

I pressed the sixth button. The boiling mirror pieces turned into lava that stayed stationary.

"Press the seventh button!" yelled David.

I hesitated. I turned around and looked at David.

"What if the lava flows towards us?" I tried to justify my hesitation.

"Then, you'll press the second button and the shield will protect us…. Come on… we've come this far."

I looked at the seventh button on the keychain. I pressed it!

Within seconds, the lava changed its shape and hardened into a dark black rock. It looked like the mirror on the wall, but with a rock consistency.

"Let it cool," David said as he approached the mirror.

"It's steaming," I added as I closely watched the lava rock mirror.

"I can't believe this key chain did all of this!" I continued.

"We can totally use this against Tibeno," David thought out loud. "Can you show me where you got it from? I want to see if we can get more."

I showed David how to get to the secretive room with lava flowing above it and the special rocks.

"Just be careful. After you pick up a rock, you need to let it go because lava will fall over it," I added.

"Don't worry. I won't touch the rock if it has lava all over it," added David.

David went to the other room.

I put the keychain on my belt. The mirrors in the room made my head spin. Each one showed a different region of the world. I went back to the mirror that showed my house. Nothing had changed. The black box was still on top of the porch. I turned my head over to the right and saw the mirror with a view of Downtown Los Angeles.

The skyscrapers looked as tall as those in New York, but much less in quantity then those in New York. I walked over to the Los Angeles mirror. As I looked into the mirror, something looked odd on the roof of the Bank of America building. I zoomed in to see what was on the roof top.

"David!" I yelled as I ran towards the other room.

"What happened!" exclaimed David as he came out of the passage leading to the other room.

"There's a black box on top of the Bank of America building in Downtown," I said.

"I'll have Amber and Robbie look into it," David said calmly.

"That's fine, but this is a different type of black box," I explained. "This black box now has red stripes on it. Do you think it's a device that tries to track us?"

"We have to call Robbie and Amber. Is the one on your house flashing red too?" asked David. "I'm going to go grab the rock. It should be ready now."

David quickly ran into the other room.

276

He came out of the room within moments. His face was as white as snow as he held a rectangular box, the same as the one on my house and the Bank of America building. Tibeno must have had my father take the boxes out before my father tried to take off the diamond while under Tibeno's mind control.

"This isn't the only one," David said as he looked at the black box he was holding in his hands.

"Why are the ones in the mirror flashing red? Both the black box on the Bank of America building and the one on my house are flashing red," I added.

"It says here on the side.... *Press red button to activate explosive*," David read carefully.

"Try and get in touch with Robbie and I'll try to contact Amber. They need to make sure no one is at my house. We need to stop the explosion in Downtown! They need to deactivate the explosive!"

We left the small box in the room and ran out of the room.

CHAPTER TWENTY-THREE

When we arrived at the Bank of America building, nothing seemed unusual. It looked like any other work day for the people walking towards the building. It was already lunch time and a lot of people were leaving the building.

"We need to get them out of here!" I exclaimed.

"I'll tell Security…. Just move everyone out," added David.

David ran to the security desk.

"There's a bomb in the building!" I yelled.

David turned around and looked at me when I yelled. So much for being subtle, I didn't want to wait for Security to sound the alarm.

Everyone started running out of the building while David explained to Security that there is a bomb on the roof. Within moments after David's explanation, Security activated the building's alarms. The alarms wailed louder than the screaming voices of the panicky crowds inside the building.

As I tried to quickly walk towards David, I saw Tibeno, at least I thought it was Tibeno.

The man was casually walking outside. He had long hair tied back in a pony tail. I remember my mom showing me a picture of Tibeno when he was younger. The face of this man was an older version of the picture she had showed me. While the man walked away, I noticed that there was a red star on his neck. He turned his head and looked at me. The man gave me a deathly stare and a grin.

It was him! It was Tibeno!

"David! Tibeno is here! Follow me!" I telepathically told David.

I ran out of the building to make sure I did not lose sight of Tibeno amidst the crowds of people leaving the building. The alarms started to sound. People were screaming as they were chaotically running to safety. I was starting to lose sight of Tibeno. I wanted to fly, but if I did, everyone would know that I'm different. I had to focus on trying to keep my distance close to Tibeno.

"How do you know it's him?" David asked as he found me among the crowd.

"He has a red star on his neck and he looks like the picture my mom showed me," I answered.

"Quick, he's going inside the car!" I exclaimed.

Tibeno entered a black sedan with tinted windows.

"Don't worry, I'll catch up to him," David said as he started running faster.

David managed to catch up to the car and jumped on its roof.

"I'll take care of him!" shouted David. "Just get the bomb!"

I didn't want to leave David alone with Tibeno, but people would be killed if I didn't take care of bomb.

I quickly ran inside the building. Everyone was running down the stairs. There would be no way I would be able to climb up the stairs. I ran to the elevator and waited for it to open. There was a swarm of people in the elevator area. The elevator opened and the group of people inside were about to trample over me as they got out in great haste. I went inside and pressed the button for the last floor.

I was all alone in the elevator. The alarm's noise pierced my ears as I watched the elevator ascend one floor at a time. With my heart beating rapidly, the relatively quick elevator ride felt endless. Finally, the elevator stopped on the last floor. When I got out of the elevator, I found the stairwell leading to the roof. I climbed the metallic staircase to the roof top.

"Amber, do you know anything about the bomb?" I asked Amber telepathically.

"Yes, it's to the left of the heliport. You only have five minutes to deactivate it. Hurry!" explained Amber.

I started to panic! I had to find the bomb quickly.

There was nothing on the heliport. There were only white lines on the floor indicating where helicopters should land. Maybe it was hidden behind something to the left of the heliport. I ran around looking. I was panicking.

How did Amber know I have five minutes? It seemed like I had already wasted a couple of minutes looking aimlessly in the direction Amber had indicated. I could feel my heart beat faster.

At the left corner of the roof, next to the heliport, there was a small vent. That was the only place that I had not checked. I ran to vent. It was there! I found the black box! It was flashing red faster than it had before.

I picked up the box to determine how I would deactivate the bomb. When I turned over the box, there was an empty hole. A small battery-activated light was attached to the box that was blinking really quickly. There was nothing else in the box except for a note. The note read:

I got what I wanted!

What did he mean? I paced around the heliport.

"Oh, no! David! He's got David!" I yelled to myself.

It made sense now. Tibeno didn't care about the building. He wanted one of us so that he could get his diamond. He didn't care which one of us he kidnapped as long as it was someone who could walk on the floor of the Sancdia.

"David!" I tried calling out to David telepathically.

I couldn't hear anything from him. Did something happen? Was I too late? Why had I left David? We were a team and I abandoned him. I had to find David. I had to stop Tibeno.

I felt the burning sensation in my hands as the fire in my hands began to help me rise off of the floor. I knew where I was headed. Although Tibeno had David, this time I would make sure Tibeno would not run away.

Flying had become second nature to me by now. I moved swiftly through the air. The wind was helping me move quicker with its gentle push.

There must have been something wrong with David's powers because he would not respond to me.

I kept on trying to contact him telepathically, but nothing came of it.

I flew over the freeway going towards Mammoth. I had become too familiar with this road that once was foreign to me.

When I passed California City, I noticed Tibeno's black sedan driving quickly on the freeway. David was lying on top of the car with his hands and feet tied together. His entire body was somehow attached to the car. David was not moving an inch, even with the swift movement of the car.

I flew in front of the car. I found a few trees on the side of the road ahead of the car and set them on fire with my hands. They quickly fell to the floor.

Tibeno veered off of the road to avoid the burning fires. He didn't seem to care. It was like an obstacle course for him. All he cared about was getting to his diamond.

The car was moving quickly, but I could fly faster. I thought that if I flew over the car, I could grab David off of the car. As I descended, something

284

stopped me from getting close to David. It was almost as if a force field was pushing me away from him.

David laid there helpless.

"Katrina, I can't use any of my powers!"

"I don't know what's going on...," he continued.

I flew down next to the car. Tibeno had attached a magnetic contraption that seemed to deactivate David's powers and have him stay stuck to the car. Tibeno looked at me. He pressed the gas pedal to go faster.

"Don't worry David.... I have a plan."

The road ahead was simply an empty desert. The only things that could be seen were the numerous Joshua trees and dry shrubs. There were no cars in sight. I decided to create a ring of fire. I began to set all the trees and shrubs on fire to encircle the speeding car.

Tibeno veered off the road again to avoid my path of fire. I began to set everything behind him on fire, just in case he tried to turn back. Since I moved more quickly than him, I burned an oval ring of fire surrounding the car, with Tibeno stuck in the middle.

Once Tibeno realized he was trapped, he jumped out of the moving car.

David was still on the car! He still could not move!

I took out the keychain that was on my belt. I pointed it at the car and pressed the number two. A shield trapped the moving car and turned off the car. I no longer needed to worry that the car would be headed into the fire. I flew next to the car.

"Hold on David! There's a magnet inside the car that's pinning you down. It's stopping your powers."

The key chain was going to come in handy again. I landed next to the car and took out the special keychain. I pointed the keychain directly at the magnet. I pressed the button to make the magnet boil.

"Ah! That's hot!" yelled David.

"Stop it! Katrina!" he continued.

I did not realize that David would feel the heat of the boiling magnet through the car. My heart started to race as I quickly pressed the button that cooled down the magnet and turned it into a lava rock.

The magnet fell onto the backseat of the car. David started to move up off the car like a caterpillar, since he was still tied up.

Tibeno grabbed me from behind. He was trying to stop me from getting to David. He put both arms around me in a bear hug such that I was not able to move.

"Do you really think I'm going to let you help him?... Huh?" asked Tibeno maliciously.

His embrace was so strong that I felt my bones crack each time he tightened his grip on me. I panted as I tried to get out of the bear hug. Tibeno was much larger than me and was able to carry me off the ground.

"I haven't come this far for you to try and stop me now," he continued.

"Why are you doing this?" I asked. I could see David slowly being able to free himself.

"I'm doing this because Amber's my daughter. Your father took her away from me and gave her to another Minder family in San Francisco. He told me that I was a Mutineer and that I could not be in a relationship with a Minder. Our marriage was not official as far as he was concerned. Yes, I was in love with your mother and made mistakes, but I had moved on and was intimate with a Minder. He banished my love's powers and took away my daughter! Your father ruined my life!" he complained.

"You're lying!" I yelled.

"And, what if I'm not?" he said sternly as he squeezed me tighter.

"I'm going to get that diamond and show him who's really in power," continued Tibeno with a maniacal chuckle.

"Never!" I yelled as I jerked my body backwards trying to free myself.

"You're going to fly me out of here," commanded Tibeno as he squeezed my body so tightly that I felt more of my bones crack.

"Aye!" I cried while forcefully holding back my tears from the pain of my arm's bones breaking.

I felt a jolt from behind.

David had freed himself!

He pushed Tibeno so fiercely that I fell to the ground because Tibeno reluctantly released his arms from the immense force. My arms were in such pain that I finally let go of my tears.

"I'm sorry Katrina.... I had to do it," David whispered when bending over to make sure I was alright.

David jumped over me and grabbed Tibeno with one arm. Tibeno could not move.

"This is enough Tibeno!" yelled David with his charismatic and overpowering voice. "You've done too much damage already."

David grabbed both of Tibeno's arms and pulled him towards the car. Tibeno was no match for

David's sheer strength. The rope that had tied up David was on the floor next to the car. He picked up the rope without releasing Tibeno from his hold and tied him up within seconds. Tibeno lay next to the car with his arms and legs tied.

"I'm not done!" Tibeno yelled. "I'm not done!"

"I've made sure that there are more like me out there!" Tibeno continued to shout sadistically. "They are my Mutineers! I've made sure to create my army!"

David ran over to me and carried me over to Tibeno. All I could feel was the pain of my broken bones. Tibeno's yelling was merely a nuisance to all the pain that I felt.

"I wish I didn't have to do this to you," said David softly. "We have to take away Tibeno's powers for good. You're going to have to try to use your hands."

"I can't," I cried. The pain was overwhelming.

"It's our only way to do it," David said as he gently placed me next to Tibeno, who was tied up.

"Hold onto my hand. It will be very quick. I promise," David said convincingly while staring at me with his beautifully long eyelashes.

David gently held both of my hands. He was careful about not making my arms move so that I wouldn't feel any pain.

"Close your eyes to lessen the pain of your arms."

"I don't think anything can lessen the pain, but let's just do this."

I felt a heavy wind encircling us. I looked down at my hands and saw the beautiful stream of golden stars coming out of David and my hands and onto Tibeno's soul. Red flashes of lightening sporadically came out of Tibeno as he screamed, "No!" and "Never!"

The golden stars stopped flowing out of our hands. It was over. Tibeno was, at last, banished. He no longer had powers or would remember any of the secrets of the Protectins. The red star disappeared from Tibeno's neck. He was now human and not a threat to the world.

Tibeno was unconscious from the impact of the banishment.

"Do you think Tibeno is really Amber's father?" I asked David.

"I don't think so. I'm sure he was lying so that you would help him. I wouldn't worry about it," said David.

"We can't tell Amber," I told David. "We have to keep this a secret. Promise?"

"Yeah… sure," agreed David.

"I also think we need to pick another Council," I continued.

"Yeah. I can't trust them. If some of them already betrayed us, who says the others won't also?" added David.

"Can you fly us out of here with your arms like that?" asked David.

"No, I can't even move them," I replied. "I do have the keychain though. You can turn the burning shrubs and trees into lava rock."

David took the keychain off my belt. He pointed them at the burning trees while walking towards them. Once the trees had turned into lava rocks, David pushed them over with his magnificent strength. One by one, David cleared a path for us to get out of the oval ring of fire.

He moved Tibeno's car to the side of the road.

"Check to make sure there isn't anything unusual in there," I told David.

I had to sit and watch because my arms were badly injured.

David threw out any electronic equipment into what was left of the dwindling fire on the opposite end of where I sat. He carried Tibeno into the car.

"Once he wakes up, he won't know what happened," added David.

"I'm so happy it's over," I said to David.

"Don't move your arms. I'm going to carry you back," David said as he picked me up off the floor.

"Thanks… I don't think I could fly home this time." I smiled.

CHAPTER TWENTY-FOUR

Jack thought I was very lucky to only have a broken left arm. My right arm was bruised, but nothing was broken. I wore cast on my left arm to help it heal.

The black box at my house was also an empty box with a light in it. Amber and Robbie figured that out after I discovered the fact that the black box on the Bank of America building was a fake. I was glad that my house was still intact.

My parents were fine too. They didn't recall the day they were trapped in the avalanche of rocks. I had Jack sprinkle some memory powder on them so that they would not remember. I did not want to relive everything that Tibeno had put them through that day. It was over and I did not have any desire to have them recall that tragic day.

Robbie and Amber were getting together over the weekends so that they would perfect their powers. Amber would drive to Jack's house and spend the day in the control room or the Dome with Robbie. I think it was only a good excuse for Amber to see Robbie. She couldn't stop talking about him!

Brenda was Brenda, as usual. She wouldn't leave David alone. I did not even have a chance to eat with David. She would shove me over and sit next to him. I had enough of her! David, on the other hand, seemed to enjoy the attention. He would often dismiss any thought that Brenda was being mean to me. I think he must have been blind to her devious tactics.

I was walking over to my class after lunch. I had reached the quad when all of the books in my right hand fell on the floor.

"Here… I'll help you," said a really handsome guy.

"Oh… sure," I said almost blushing.

The boy had brown curly hair with strands of blond highlights glistening in the sun.

He picked up all of my books.

"You know…. I can walk you to class," he said. "I don't want you hurting anything else."

He looked at the cast on my left arm. He grinned slightly, only to convince me to agree to his proposed act of chivalry.

"Um… sure… thanks," I said blushing.

"My name's Katrina," I continued. "I didn't catch your name."

"Oh…. I'm Oliver, a sophomore Psych major."

"I don't want to be forward, but do you want to go out this Saturday night?" asked Oliver. "We can meet at the quad Saturday night at five."

"Well… I don't really know you," I replied.

"What do you want to know? I'll tell you everything," he smiled.

"Come on… what do you say?" asked Oliver with a very convincing grin.

"Um…," I paused for a moment. "Sure," I said blushing. "I guess we can have some coffee at night at the Samuelson Pavilion. I mean… I kind of want to get to know you first before we go anywhere."

"I'll take anything." He smiled.

"I have to go to class. You really don't need to carry my book."

"I need to make sure you're intact before we have our date on Saturday night."

"You mean, our 'getting to know each other coffee time'."

"Whatever you want to call it." He laughed.

I started to feel uneasy, almost like I was cheating on David. I guess, you could call it a date with Oliver. In some ways, I wanted this. David had been busy entertaining both Brenda and me that it was probably about time for me to move on. I didn't like having to fight for David's attention.

Oliver and I arrived at my class.

"That was really nice of you," I said to Oliver as he handed me my books in front of my class.

"I'll see you on Saturday for our 'getting to know each other coffee date'," said Oliver as he winked and walked away from the class.

"Who was that?" asked David furiously. He had come to class from the opposite direction.

"Oh… he's Oliver. He asked me out this Saturday," I bragged.

"And you said 'no' right?" added David.

"Of course not! I'm meeting him on Saturday night. It's not like you're my boyfriend," I hinted to David.

"I don't trust him," continued David with his jealous rage. "You can't go out with him because…"

"Because what?" I added.

"Because you don't even know him," said David frustrated. "I care about you and I don't want you to get hurt. Besides, I really like you and I don't want you to go out with anyone else," added David.

"What about Brenda?" I asked.

"Brenda? I've known Brenda since we were five years old," he said. "She's always been all over me! Don't you think I'd be going out with her by now if I liked her?"

David tried to put his hand on my shoulder. I quickly pushed him off of me.

"If you like me so much than why don't you show it!" I yelled with tears streaming down my eyes.

"I do! But, you always seem to doubt yourself," he said upset. "I really do like you and I want to be with you and no one else, not even Brenda!"

David put his hands around my shoulder and hugged me.

"Please… you can't do this to me Katrina! You're a part of me… you can't go out with that guy," continued David.

He looked at me while gently stroking my arm.

"I don't trust him. I just don't," added David. "I promise… I'll stop talking to Brenda. Please… I don't want to lose you."

I cried and finally hugged back David. He was so sincere in his plea. Perhaps I was letting my jealousy get in the way of what David actually felt of me. I didn't want to lose him. At the same time, I didn't want him to let Brenda shorten my time with him by taking away all of his attention.

"I don't want to lose you too…" I finally said with a tear falling from one of my eyes.

He wiped the tear.

"Never," he said as he kissed me on my cheek.

He took my books and held my only uninjured hand into class.

I turned and looked at Oliver walking away in the distance. Something red seemed to glisten on his neck. I'm sure it was my imagination. I don't think he could be a Mutineer. Maybe, David had a point. Maybe, Oliver wasn't who he said he was…. I had to find out.

**

"I was part of the volcano and all of its fury."

ABOUT THE AUTHOR

Talin Mari is an author and blogger of Armenian descent who lives in the United States. Ever since she was a young girl, she was fascinated by all of the art of storytelling. She remembers being inspired to write as a result of a school contest in the second grade.

Talin Mari believes that writing is the road to escape the realty of everyday life, while reading it is the destination. She writes because she wants to be heard. She wants to be the voice that fills a void.

The Diamond Guardians is the first book in *The Diamond Guardians Series*.

Website www.TalinMari.com

Blog site www.TalinMariBlogs.com

Facebook Talin Mari – Writer

Twitter @TalinMariWriter